Don't Blame the Yeti

A hair-raising Himalayan hike

Tess Burrows

Lightning
Books

Published in 2020
by Lightning Books Ltd
Imprint of EyeStorm Media
312 Uxbridge Road
Rickmansworth
Hertfordshire
WD3 8YL

www.lightning-books.com

British Library Cataloguing in Publication Data
A catalogue record for this book is available from the British Library.

Printed by CPI Group (UK) Ltd, Croydon CR0 4YY

ISBN: 9781785632075

With love
for my grand-daughter Lyra
and the children of the world,
that they may see the magic…

Invitation from Honey Angel

Dear Reader,

Would you be excited to go on an adventure knowing you might meet the Yeti — the mythical beast of the high Tibetan plateau?

Then, this story is for you.

Yup, you might think the Yeti scary, but he is like the amazing monster in your mind, an inner Yeti perhaps, who sees all things as you would love to see them — flawless...enchanting...awe-inspiring...

And, like all magic, it's not whether he exists that's important but the believing in him...!! This holds your dreams. Makes life fun and intriguing. Helps you create things. And pushes you further than you thought you could go...

So, I invite you to pause with wonder along the way of this story, and also along the way of your life... To feel the magic. To know the love. To see further...

But, whatever happens, don't blame the yeti!

See you along the way...

HONEY ANGEL

ANGELIC REALM

1

The New Apprentice

Something was astir in the angelic realm. A new arrival. Unusual rowdiness…

"Jumpin' jellyfish!! What on Earth's going on?"

"Nope, not 'on Earth', but you're safe now," Honey Angel smiled comfortingly, her silky gown and long raven hair shimmering like candles on a cake.

Her new apprentice had arrived.

She soothed his shock, talking with her honeyed voice until he grew calm and focused enough to notice that behind her he could see large golden wings.

"Are you an angel?"

"Yup."

"Coolish!" He glanced behind him hopefully to see if by some miracle he'd acquired wings too, but was disappointed. "Am I an angel?"

A honeyed giggle was all that came back to him.

The new apprentice didn't remember much before that: long black claws dragging him along the ground. And fear – a whole load of fear. Then his mind yawning as though someone had just pressed the TV remote on all the channels at once. An explosion of colour. A very bright light. Then blackness. Nothing else. Till a gentle voice was saying "he's awake". And many pairs of shining eyes were looking down at him in a kindly, loving way.

"Uh-oh!… So if this is where angels live… where am I?"

"You're in Angelic Realm School."

"School? That's for kids and fishes. Not my sort of thing."

"School for guides."

"But I'm only…"

"We know what you are. You've done well and

worked hard on your character. You deserve this opportunity to help humans."

"Uh-oh!..."

"Yup. And as my apprentice you'll learn new skills. I'll teach you to be a guide – an invisible guide. We have an important mission for you."

"Jumpin' jellyfish!"

The training started the next day. Well, soon after anyway, as everything seemed to be without any sense of time. He found he could speed things up or slow them down just by thinking them so. It was confusing, but fun.

"You need to try to keep a sense of the time that humans use," Honey Angel said, her face shining with loveliness. "That way you'll find them easier to work with. Why don't you concentrate on what's happening and not worry about past or future? It makes things happier."

The new apprentice was puzzled. It wasn't easy to forget how he felt – the fear of something really scary, even though the memory of what it actually was seemed to have disappeared. Come to think of it he couldn't even remember who he was...

"Don't worry," Honey Angel comforted. "Who you were isn't important. It's now that matters. You'll soon get the hang of it. I'll be here to help you." She wrapped a wing softly around his shoulders. (If you've ever been hugged by an angel you'll know it makes you feel utterly loved…)

So the new apprentice relaxed. Here he was with his own enchanting angel on tap. What more could anyone ask for?

"Firstly, I want you to practise thinking thoughts to create things," she said, her golden eyes sparkling. "This is much easier here than on the Earth Realm. Most humans take a very long time to get it. So…take a deep breath and let go of any worries. Then see yourself as calm and peaceful, and imagine something lovely, like…floating on a serene sea at sunset."

That was easy. Also, it was fun. Before long he was ducking between waves and spotting darting silver fish, watching little bubbles of sparkling air. It was very real. He felt supremely happy.

"Well done. Good try. Though more control would be good," said Honey Angel. "And remember, helping humans has to come from being steady; otherwise it won't work."

"Right, I'm ready. I can do this!" He had no idea what 'this' was but felt so full of joy it didn't matter.

"Okay. Now…we need to practise what's called shifting. You need to move your awareness down into the solid Earth Realm. It has to be done through an egg-of-light."

"A what?"

"An egg-of-light! It's the most useful thing you'll

learn. It can help any situation... In this case helping you shift. How you do it is by surrounding yourself with love, and then seeing it as light. Start off imagining it and just let it happen."

"Uh-oh!..."

"Go on...make yourself an egg-of-light."

The new apprentice tried imagining the love he felt when being hugged by Honey Angel. Then painting it with sunshine colour, and finally moulding it into an egg-shape around him.

"Easy! Well done. Then set the trigger word, 'tumble-rumble', and simply imagine exactly where you want to be. Hold my hand. We'll do it together this time. There's a human I want you to meet. You'll be her invisible guide. She'll be the only one able to hear you. All in her mind."

There was a sensation a bit like jumping out of a plane – sort of somersaulting. And barely had he said "tumble-rumble" than he felt Honey Angel drag him along to a city marketplace.

The air seemed heavy on the Earth Realm. It was raining.

They watched...

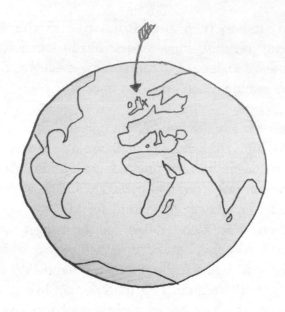

EARTH REALM

2

Torma's Promise

A beautiful, dark-haired girl sat wide-eyed on a stool, listening to a story. It was about escaping across the mountains and it was told by a young man at the back of his market stall in London, grey, busy and traffic-ridden as usual. The girl loved living here because it was her home city. And now it was his too.

"The scary thing," the young man, Tenzin, was saying, "is that being hunted freezes your heart."

The rain was pouring down in buckets, making a deafening noise on the awning above them. He'd added heavy plastic to cover most of the enticing things for sale. Normally the girl liked looking at them, with their colours of chocolate, muted gold and rust reminding her of treasure. But few people were venturing out to buy today. It was a perfect time to listen. He wrapped her in a soft shawl, patterned like his wool jacket, and talked. It was as though the time had come for his heartbreaking story to be set free.

"The dark was so...so...bitter, Squirt," he said. "I couldn't see the mountains rising steeply up, but felt the cold as it rolled down, engulfing me like an avalanche. My choice was either the dangerous slope or bullets from the Invader soldiers chasing me. Then I came across a narrow crack deep in the snow and I managed to hide. If found I'd have been trapped. Even then I couldn't lie down and shut my eyes, for the cold would've brought certain death to a sleeping body..."

The girl was enthralled with the terror of this real-life adventure, not least because he'd been twelve years old. The age she was now – able to do nearly everything for herself, though admittedly still scared of being alone.

She loved Tenzin like the big brother she'd never

had, partly because he insisted on fondly calling her Squirt. She preferred it to her real name, Torma. Kids at school would always tease her and say "Here comes Storma Cry-baby. Watch out for the angry rain!" She knew she cried a lot. She couldn't help it, but wished she'd been called something cool like Elsie or Bess… She just wanted to be accepted by the other kids.

As he talked it was as if she was there with him. She could feel the snow on her boots kicking each step…and sense the icy wind on her cheeks, trying to keep an exhausted, starving body alive. And then there was the hiding and the listening to something dreadful that he couldn't talk about.

She didn't want to know about that bit anyway.

What bothered her was the way Tenzin now kept looking around at the dark shadows behind the canvas of the market stall. It was impossible to tell if perhaps there was someone there listening too. Why would he be worried about that? It made her jumpy.

Yet there was something about his moon-like face and the surprising calm smile in his eyes that seemed to connect them and hug her deep inside with the feeling that all was well.

She'd hung out with him many times after school when her Granny, who she lived with, went to buy food, and she always begged to be allowed to stay with him, but this was the only time he poured his heart out. It made her feel important. And she loved him even more for it.

She moved the stool closer to the comfort of his body and strained to hear above the noise of the rain. She didn't want to miss a thing he said.

"After the escape I badly wanted to go back, Squirt, but dared not because I'd promised my mother I never would. She told me, 'You'll find freedom and education... If you come back to our country, now occupied by Invader soldiers, you'll be put in prison and tortured...and your family as well. Those that have escaped are always severely dealt with.'"

Torma didn't understand why Invaders would treat local people so badly, or what it would be like being told never to come home. She just knew she'd never want to leave Granny, her only family, like that.

"So why would you ever *want* to go back?" she asked.

"I need to know now, after ten years, that the heart of my country still beats. My country is my land, my family... It's part of me." He tapped his hand fiercely on his chest. "I need to feel it, Squirt."

She nodded. She felt his pain. Somehow she recognised it.

"And another reason..." he said intensely.

She looked up. Surely there couldn't be anything

else as important.

He went on, "I also made a promise to my tiny sister that I haven't kept."

"But you were only twelve at the time," she said, knowing full well that age was no excuse for breaking a promise.

"Not too young to know the way of my people –"

She raised her eyebrows questingly.

"– That if there is opportunity to help someone, without hurting others, then it must be done."

"Tell me…"

"Well, you might think it's foolish."

"It's okay. Tell me," she insisted.

"I've never told anyone…"

"Go on…" It not only made her feel special; it made her want to help.

"All right," he glanced furtively over his shoulder. "Well, I loved my sister dearly. When she was tiny she was frail and I was always looking for gifts to make her smile… I'm not sure I want to tell you this…"

She kept quiet, sensing there was something he needed to get off his chest. So she tried to be accepting, like a pet hamster, so he would feel safe enough to bring up what he needed to say.

"Okay, well… One day when my family were visiting some foreigner's camp I found a soft-toy penguin…and…I stole it!"

"You stole a penguin?" She laughed.

"Well, the old people of my land don't believe that 'stuff' is important like in the Western world. And things sort of belong to everyone. So I took this penguin I'd been allowed to play with, put him on our nomad cart and brought him home to our tent for my tiny sister.

"Oh, I see."

"But I never felt right about it."

"You did it because you wanted to help your tiny sister."

"Yes, the intent was good. But others may have got hurt in the process. It seemed a very special penguin. As though it had heart."

"And your sister loved it?"

"Yes, she was inseparable from it. Till the fateful day of the raid."

"What raid?"

"Invader soldiers came to take our livestock – our yaks, sheep and horses. They said they had instructions to move us into a nice new home in a town. My father was very angry. There was a fight. He was hit hard on the head with the butt of a gun. I never saw him after that. The soldiers took him away."

She stared at Tenzin, still not understanding but feeling his heartache. She tucked the shawl tighter around her shoulders as if it would help.

"During the fight my mother hid with my tiny

sister in a dry river-bed and something happened in there that spooked them. My mother wouldn't say what. But during the chaos my sister lost the penguin."

"How?"

"I dunno. She said it was some sort of an animal that took it."

"Oh!"

"She was distraught... I promised I'd find it for her. But after that my mother could think of nothing else but getting me away before the Invader soldiers came back. She sent me to my uncle's camp with a message that I was to join a group crossing the mountains. That was when she made me promise not to come back. And never to get in touch..."

She could see Tenzin's eyes glistening with tears. How must it've been? Could she go through pain and fear like that?

She felt that was all he was going to say. He looked drained. His story had been wrought from deep within himself.

Could there be a reason she had to hear this? Could she help him? Without hurting others, of course.

A voice came into her head.

There's always some way to help.

He needed to search for the heart of his country, and for a lost penguin. He couldn't go back across the mountains. But…but…perhaps someone else could do it for him… Maybe she could be that someone…? The thought made her feel both excited and scared. Certainly there was longing…

They carried the same blood, she and Tenzin. He was Tibetan – from the magical land of Tibet, across the great Himalayan mountains. Her Granny was Tibetan. Did that make them family? Certainly that made her a quarter Tibetan. Were her roots calling her?

While her mind was thinking, her mouth just blurted out, "Tenzin, I'll go back for you, across the mountains. I'll search. Find the answers. I promise."

"It'd be dangerous, Squirt…"

"I'm not afraid," her mouth lied.

His smile sealed her promise, though she had no idea how such an impossible thing could ever happen.

3

Moonbeam Music

"See how easy it is to be a voice in her head," Honey Angel said.

"Jumpin' jellyfish!" said the new apprentice doubtfully. "She didn't even know we were standing right next to her."

"Well, that's a good thing," said Honey Angel. "Think how scared she'd have been if she knew.

Once she's used to you things'll be different."

"She didn't reply."

"Nope, but she heard your words, There's always some way to help, and it affected her promise."

"Uh-oh!..."

"I must admit I did give her a little angelic sparkle as well."

"Coolish! How did you do that?"

"That's an advanced technique...known as moonbeam music...but let's just get the basics sorted first shall we? Next time I want you to implant the words by yourself."

"But what if I get them wrong and mess up?"

"So long as you always do your work with love, seeing an egg-of-light...then you can't go wrong. And anyway, human kids are very good at hearing voices in their heads – unlike their adults. They think of them as imaginary playmates."

Honey Angel put a shiny wing lovingly around his shoulder.

"C'mon, let's shift and listen carefully to our girl's thoughts. We'll learn what's going on and where we can help."

EARTH REALM

4

Forbidden

Oh poo…! Torma was thinking.

She had to speak to Granny about her promise to go to Tibet, but had no idea how to do it. Even though Granny was Tibetan, she knew it would be difficult.

She usually didn't listen when Granny explained about the family and why she was part-Tibetan.

It made her feel she didn't belong anywhere. Like being lost. Yet Granny would always tell her anyway in her kind and gentle way – except when Torma made her cross, and then she'd go red in the face and swear bringing up her grand-daughter tested her self-control to the limit. But she'd soon recover.

Torma knew Granny was loving, or compassionate as the Tibetans call it – the sort of person who, on finding a slug in the lettuce on her plate of food, rather than screaming and throwing it down the toilet, would pick it up carefully, saying, 'Oh you poor sweet thing, have you lost your way?' and carry it outside to place in a window-box full of flowers – usually the neighbour's one, as Granny didn't have a window-box.

Hmmm, agreeing to a trip to Tibet might need more than compassion for slugs.

Torma's thoughts rambled uncertainly through the family history, wondering how it might help her promise:

My great-grandparents came out of Tibet over the mountains with thousands escaping after the invasion. Hmmm, maybe crossing the mountains is in our blood. Came to England... their daughter was Granny...who grew up to marry an Englishman called Grandpa...settled in London. That's why I live here.

Then the story gets really sad, she thought. They

only had one child, my mother…death of Grandpa from heart-attack broke Granny's heart…so she retreated into not going out much…worse when my mother became pregnant and died soon after my birth…never knew why… So Granny brought me up…typical English upbringing, fish and chips, that sort of thing…though Granny's so fiercely proud of being Tibetan she often speaks to me in the Tibetan language…and tells me yeti tales… I love her dearly… But, annoyingly, my family history makes me feel different from other kids at school.

For one thing, other kids know who their father is – even those who don't actually live with him. Nobody tells me about my dad, and I can't keep asking Granny 'cos, on this bit of the family, she always goes into a silent sulk. He must have done something really bad for her not to tell me. I don't know if he's alive. I don't know if he's Tibetan – can't tell from my looks. Granny always says I take after my English grandpa, but with high Tibetan cheekbones, though kids at school tease me about my narrow eyes and mountain skin.

Torma sniffled. Tears were welling up.

I always feel different from them, she thought, like something important is missing… Maybe it's 'cos I don't have a parent to take me to exciting activities I want to do, like gymnastics or hamster classes – just a granny, who doesn't even drive… I stay in my room for hours every day and read adventure books...love reading... But I feel I've missed out on having fun. Too shy to make friends anyway. Luckily I'm always able to talk to playmates in my head. They're always on my side. They don't mind if I'm not brave...

It didn't all add up to much chance of Granny taking her to Tibet.

She thought she heard then:

You're fery frave. It'd fe foolish fo fo across the fountains.

Maybe it was another mind playmate in her head being an idiot. More likely it was the wind.

But the voice went on.

Imagine the end fesult fith all your fight...

"Go away," said Torma. If it was a new playmate, it sounded too stupid. If it wasn't, it was just annoying.

But it persisted.

Fon't forry 'fout fow it's foing to fappen. The fetails fill fort femselves out. Frust the froccess.

Save me! she thought. That's all I need: a brainless playmate with a lisp...

She talked about it during break-time at school with the one friend she did have, another misfit, a girl with goofy teeth and glasses named Violet. She was the only one who knew about the playmates in Torma's head.

"Why don't you ask the new one what his name is?" she said.

"'Cos I've always called each one LangLang, the only name I could say as a baby, which stuck," Torma said. "So with an f letter lisp this one would have to be FangFang. Not sure I can live with a playmate called FangFang!" They both collapsed in giggles.

"Maybe he's speaking in code," Violet said. "Fee, Fi, Foe, Fum – like a giant!… Maybe he's really coolish."

"Coolish? Coolish, not foolish… Yay, Vi!!. You could be right… It's an f letter code. Listen… 'It'd be coolish to go across the mountains. Imagine the end result with all your might.' We've got it!!! And so I have to imagine the journey in my mind travelling over big mountains. And feel it inside." She danced up and down with excitement. "How clever is that!!"

"Don't see how that's going to work," Violet said.

"Me neither, but FangFang said 'trust the process'…"

Violet giggled. Then looked concerned. "How d'you know you even *should* listen to him?"

"I don't." Torma shrugged. "But I like what he

says… I'm imagining the journey, over and over, with all my might. And it'd definitely be coolish to go across the mountains…"

"Anyway, how're you going to do that? You're far too young."

"Well, Tenzin did it at age twelve. I just know that's what I want to do… I feel it inside me."

Violet giggled again and they played attacking aliens on the swinging bars until the end of break-time.

Granny always met Torma after school to walk back home to their flat, a cosy little two-bedroomed place overlooking tiny gardens at the back. She loved it, as it was their hideaway from the world – just her and Granny – though sometimes she'd see Granny looking wistful saying, "One day we'll have open spaces and freedom," and she wouldn't understand, but it would set up a yearning in her for something she couldn't grasp.

Today Granny met her at the gate with her usual enveloping hug. She wore the same long dress she'd worn for as long as Torma could remember, with her grey-streaked black hair braided and tied up with what looked like a bone, and a simple necklace of bright-coloured stones. She looked exceptionally happy.

"What is it, Granny?" Torma asked as they walked, even before "What's for supper?"

"We're having visitors. My sweet sister-in-law, Ani, and her friend Yuhu, great-aunts to you, are coming over to stay. They're not Tibetan. They're from Hong Kong, but have some special work preparing for a journey into Tibet in a few weeks. I'm sure they'll be no trouble, but you'll have to move into my bedroom with me. Hope you don't mind?"

FangFang's voice, was jumping up and down in Torma's head. She had trouble listening to Granny and him at the same time. He was trying to blurt out:

Fee fow easy it is?

It took all of five seconds for the penny to drop. Her great-aunts were going to Tibet. Would they go over the mountains? Would they take her with them?

She tried to look normal.

Granny looked pointedly at her. Torma had forgotten that the person who brought her up and knew her better than anyone in the world, would sense she too was excited inside.

"No Granny, 'course I don't mind," she said, and rushed on ahead.

How could I mind? she thought, though I wouldn't want to leave Granny...and would she let me go with them?

Anyhow it all seemed too good to be true. Was there an angel conspiring to make things work in a certain way?

It seemed so, even though she'd never spoken to an angel. But she had always felt she might do so one day. After all, she spoke with mind playmates often enough, and they always talked about angels. This day was turning out to be exciting!

Incredibly, Granny was in such a good mood that she suggested going to play in the park. How often did that happen! Cool!!! Torma went running and jumping and FangFang dared her to go for the hardest challenges, like leaping over a muddy pond and climbing a dodgy fence, as though they'd been best friends all their lives. It was impossible to feel alone with him around. But in spite of the recklessness, she felt she should trust him.

Even so, she ended up cross with herself for falling out of the fairy tree where, according to FangFang, a lot of nature fairies hung out. And how was she to explain to Granny about the tear in her school uniform, the blood all over her leg and the frog-like state of her hair? Well, the uniform shouldn't be a dress, she thought. She liked baggy hoodies, long shorts and bare feet. School was the only time she ever wore a dress, outside dire emergencies – like Granny saying she couldn't have ice cream unless she did.

FangFang came in:

Your fardian angel fill always fook after you. Angels, fike fature fairies, fan felp fith fings. Fey fan fix fings. You fave to ask fem for felp.

So! You have to ask angels for help...

She felt better about herself after that and asked him again about going across the mountains.

Yeah, he said. Fometimes fen fomebody fictures a fappening fith all feir fight fe angels felp fife along in a fay fat fakes everything fit fogether.

Hmmm... It seemed this was one of those times. Yay!

That night Granny sat down on Torma's bed to say goodnight. "Well, my sweet girl. Come on, spit it out. What's on your mind?"

"Nothing. What...?" Torma was taken aback. She'd thought she was acting as normal as a slug at a picnic.

"Tell me!"

Well, she thought, all I have to do is persuade Granny. So may as well start now. She blurted out, "I want to go to Tibet."

A thin veil of sadness spread over Granny. "Torma-la, you can't do that. It's out of the question. What would I do without you? And anyway it'd cost a huge amount of money, which we don't have."

"But you've always told me to do what my

heart says and follow my dreams."

"Sensible dreams, yes. Tibet, no! Tibet would bring nothing but pain. No!

"But Granny, Aunt Ani and Aunt Yuhu are going…'

"That's different. They have important work to do."

"But I could help them."

"It's too dangerous, No! We're not going to talk about it any more."

That was a definite decision then. She thought of Tenzin and the promise she'd made. Her heart ached. She cried herself to sleep.

ANGELIC REALM

5

School

"I messed up! Janglin' angels! I was so excited, I got the shape of the egg-of-light wrong."

"Yup, it was more a lunch-box-of-light," Honey Angel told the new apprentice, FangFang. "Rounded is stronger, and helps everything flow properly. That's why the f letter got stuck. But remember it's the intention of love that counts, and you got that right. And it'll be better next time."

"If there is a next time," he mumbled. "How would you like to be called FangFang, and laughed at?"

Honey Angel thought it was funny but didn't laugh outwardly, as she didn't want to hurt his feelings. She knew he wasn't that good at reading her thoughts. "C'mon, cheer up, you were very good at making sure she enjoyed herself in the park."

"Yeah, that was fun."

"But one of the chief angels has sent a message to say that if she hurts herself again because of your encouragement, like when she fell out of the fairy tree, then you're to be put on a gentler assignment."

FangFang fell silent.

"She was, shall we say, rescued. You have her guardian angel to thank for that."

FangFang looked up, interested. "Who's that?"

"You're looking at her."

"But you're…my teacher. How can you do that job as well?"

"It's quite possible to be in two places at once. In fact, very many places. How d'you think the chief angels manage?"

"Uh-oh!… Jumpin' jellyfish! I've got a lot to learn," said FangFang, and thought for a while…

"So why do you need me to help?"

"Just look at how well our girl listens to you. Even speaking in code. She never listens to me. It's all about vibes. You and she are in tune."

Suddenly he felt much better and ready to go back to work.

"Well done," said Honey Angel. "Let's look at the colour and quality of the vibes she gives off, telling us how she's feeling. Think vibrancy of the vibes! Listen in."

EARTH REALM

6

The Aunts

Torma felt miserable about Granny not letting her go to Tibet. Her only hope was that her aunts might think differently about her promise. She couldn't wait for them to arrive.

She wondered whether to speak to some of the kids in the playground at school. They were confident and knew how to get what they wanted. But she wasn't brave enough. She knew she'd be laughed at and called a loser as usual, making her feel small. So she talked to Violet, who said, "Forget the idea. Kids can't go and do things like that. We have to wait till we're old enough. Let's go and play aliens on the swinging bars."

Torma shook her head. She knew she did feel old enough. Even Violet didn't understand.

If it hadn't been for FangFang she might have given up the fight. After all, she didn't want to upset Granny. But he kept on and on saying:

Fings are foolish. Felieve in yourself.

"Go away. You're only a voice in my head," she moped. But it kept a tiny flame of hope alive that things might change when her aunts arrived.

Finally the day came. She hung precariously out of the bedroom window so she could see the street below, and peered down eagerly as a black London taxi drew up and two figures emerged, to be greeted by Granny draping white silk scarves around their necks – the traditional Tibetan greeting which she loved to do on special occasions. Even from her awkward vantage point, Torma could see that her aunts weren't a bit like she had expected. She'd thought they'd be tall and grim and boringly old. But they appeared to be short and round and, from the way they hugged Granny, full of energy and fun.

Having dragged their luggage up to the main

room they collapsed laughing onto the sofa as Torma peered nervously around the door. You'd have thought she was a long-lost penguin the way they jumped up, overjoyed to see her and greeting her with high-fives.

"Here…some presents from Hong Kong," said Aunt Yuhu, who was dressed in a blue jumpsuit topped by a bright-pink hat and sunglasses. She held out an equally bright cotton bag, brimming with exciting-looking parcels. A happy smile covered her whole face.

"Yay! Thank you." Torma was thrilled. She didn't often have presents.

"And some goodies from the pingpong plane," said Aunt Ani.

Torma realised her other aunt, simply dressed in jeans and a t-shirt, with a nose-stud and a tree tattoo on her arm inscribed 'Aspire to Peace', was no taller than she was. She looked straight into eyes full of warmth and love. And immediately felt safe.

So…they seemed okay.

But she needed to test them. While they washed, and Granny laid out the welcome meal, she ran outside to the neighbour's window-box and found two little black slugs underneath the dahlias. When no one was looking she managed to sneak them, one each, into the lettuce on Aunt Ani and Aunt Yuhu's salad plates… Not so much hidden slugs as can't-be-missed sort of slugs.

She watched, fascinated, as Aunt Ani put her hands out to bless the food – of interest in itself – but then noticed movement across both plates as the slugs rushed for cover (in a sluggy sort of way). Aunt Yuhu did a double-take with a big in-breath, suddenly very interested in her phone. Aunt Ani calmly picked up her slug in her fingers, studying it. "Ah. I see you have pingpong creatures like the ones we have in Hong Kong. They're eaten for protein there, but here we might put them in the flowers to hide from birds and hedgehogs."

Torma was sure the slugs enjoyed their adventure.

Granny glared at Torma.

Oh, poo! Maybe she'd blown the ice cream…

But the aunts had passed Torma's test. She liked them. They were dudey aunts!

It wasn't until a few days later that she had a good chance to speak with Aunt Ani as they walked down to the corner shop to buy some rice for Aunt Yuhu, who believed she wasn't properly fed if she didn't have rice. Now if it was ice cream…

"You've been wanting to know about our journey across the mountains, haven't you?" Aunt Ani said kindly.

Torma nodded enthusiastically.

"Well, it's a secret pingpong mission, so please don't talk about it," she said, intriguingly.

Torma had figured out that 'pingpong' was an Aunt Ani word used to give things a happy lift, so just smiled as her aunt continued.

"We've been asked to help the planet. Shady Forces have been threatening our Earth. So we're going to do something about this by changing the energy of a special pyramid-shaped mountain… known as the magic mountain. Of all places it happens to be in Tibet, the land of your ancestors, on the far side of the Himalayas. Some call it the heart of the world. This will allow good energy to come in there to be used around the world for positive things. It will overcome the Shady Forces."

"Yay! A real life battle with aliens?"

"Sort of… We'll be travelling slowly up through north-west Nepal, across pingpong mountains, following a great river to its source near the magic mountain, which we'll then walk around."

This sounded to Torma the most exciting thing she'd ever heard… Aunt Ani could sense this and went on, "I see that you have a pure heart, so I can show you how to help with your thoughts by holding us in good energy."

She could hear FangFang jumping up and down in her mind, so she giggled and told him quietly, "Just wait till the next time I'm in trouble with

Granny and I can tell her I have a pure heart."

But FangFang was shouting:

Fow! Ask fer fow!

Of course… "Please, Aunt Ani…" she implored. "Please can I come with you?"

Aunt Ani looked at her in a thinking sort of way that Torma had never experienced before. It was as though they were equals and made her feel bigger and taller.

After shopping they returned home to find Aunt Yuhu in an agitated state in the kitchen. She was pacing up and down, throwing her hands repeatedly in the air and becoming very red in the face. Torma couldn't help thinking she looked like an over-cooked beetroot.

"I've spent the entire day at the offices of our top-class travel agent," she said, with her arms emphasising the top-class, and knocking over a pan of soup in the process. "The ones we've been told we must use…"

Granny was looking worried at this unexpected flustering of her nice, well-behaved house-guests, and rushed to catch the pan.

Aunt Yuhu realised she was getting out of hand and apologised profusely. She explained, "I've paid for the airfares, the itinerary is at last all ready to go, so things can be organised in time, but they've come up with a new rule."

They all stared at her expectantly.

"I'd thought that because we're from Hong Kong there wouldn't be any problems. But they say it'll only work in Tibet if we have a group of three hikers – some recent Invader government rule. Crazy dimsims!… Just 'cos they've forcibly taken over a country, they think they're so powerful they can do what they like with tourists! If we want to go, we have no choice but to find another person to come with us."

She sat down suddenly, face in hands. "But what we're doing is so important we can't take just anybody with us. It has to be someone with a pure heart, who can learn quickly how to do our work. There's barely any time…"

"I think I have the answer," said Aunt Ani quietly, looking at Torma.

Torma looked at Granny, who looked aghast.

Aunt Ani took hold of both Granny's hands. "We could pay for Torma, because we've money left from the pingpong patron in Hong Kong who's made the whole thing possible. I do believe she's the right person. It's better to have a blank canvas to teach than one that's already blemished. And it will be useful, as she speaks Tibetan. I could talk to her school and find a way for the headmistress to understand the importance of this. We would look after her with our lives."

Torma felt she would burst with excitement.

But Granny was shaking her head.

7

The Vibe-catcher

"Jumpin' jellyfish! Did you see the bright light shining around her when she felt joy?" said FangFang, thrilled. "It was bursting out from her."

Honey Angel beamed. "Yup, that's her vibe-catcher. And did you notice it grow outwards and touch the others, which also then brightened?"

"It's like magic isn't it? How come I never

noticed the vibe-catchers before? Everyone is walking around surrounded by a bubble of their own thoughts and feelings. I love it!"

"It's just a matter of focus. All sorts of things are going on all around. It depends where you put your awareness. And like all these things, once you've noticed it once or twice it becomes normal."

"Coolish!"

"And did you see how murky and dull her vibe-catcher was when she was miserable?"

"Yeah, it made me feel like I wanted to polish it."

"Excellent! And well done for not giving up when she told you to go away. It eventually lifted her."

Honey's praise made FangFang feel that at last he was getting something right. Though he was still having trouble with the f letter getting through, especially when he got excited.

"Let's shift and watch the play of vibe-catchers. I want you to spot the light that we angels look for to put to useful purposes – our special magic."

8

Peace Penguins

"That pink jacket is revolting." said Torma. "And who needs four t-shirts and four pairs of socks?"

She didn't care about the frantic preparations taking place. Passports, visas, adventure clothes, sleeping bags, boots to test out, toothpaste – so much stuff which everyone insisted was important. And so much fuss! But she did care about Granny crying as though heartbroken (in the same way she herself had when her pet hamster had died), and finally agreeing that she could go.

So now Aunt Yuhu was able to sort the travel arrangements, saying, "The instruction from the Invader authorities to have three hikers in our group is because only then can we have an obligatory minder – a man who's to accompany us in Tibet and look after us. Hmm! More like spy on us. The last thing we want. We'll have to put up with him. But Torma is booked in now!"

Torma hugged Aunt Yuhu gratefully.

And Aunt Ani had important business to attend to with rocks. She told Torma, "We have to place special rock crystals along the way on our journey, and lay a few at a certain high point on the magic mountain. Then when we chant pingpong words and hold clear thoughts it all helps the good energy to come in."

"Like real live magic?" asked Torma.

"Yes, so long as it's done in a positive and loving way."

Torma was starstruck. she'd heard people say rock crystal work was mumbo-jumbo. She rather liked mumbo-jumbo. It was one of those subjects that made her become alive inside. Why couldn't they study mumbo-jumbo at school?

Aunt Ani showed her some clear quartz pieces and they practised washing them with salt water, committing them to positive things and then giving them set tasks. Torma asked for one to help her not to cry when things weren't going her way. So far so good…

"So they're a bit like angels – fixing things for us?" she asked.

Aunt Ani looked surprised she knew about angels. "A little bit, yes, but crystals are very scientific. They're used to hold and increase things energetically, just like in computers."

Torma nodded, as though she understood.

"Though there was a problem with the crystals we're taking with us for the journey. Some external force affected them in a negative way…"

"Shady…?" she whispered, a little scared.

"Yes, but it's fixed now. However, Torma, remember, you can always protect yourself with good energy. There's many ways of doing it and you'll find your own, but try seeing an egg-of-light around you. Go on…"

She had no problem. After all she'd spent time imagining crossing mountains… Just an egg-of-light was easy. And surprisingly, around the edges of the egg she saw golden movement…

FangFang was in her mind, all excited:

Angels, angels…fee the angels.

Yay! Cool!

Torma was determined to put her new angel-finding skill to good use.

True to her word, Aunt Ani had persuaded Torma's headteacher, Miss Potram, or Potty as the kids called her, to let Torma have time away. And she had organised an assembly with all the pupils, not only for her class but for the entire school, to write peace messages. They would take these with them to speak out on the winds of the planet from the magic mountain. It was a way they could all help peace in the world.

Potty asked Torma to stand up in front of everyone and read her message. She felt unable to do it. She was terrified. Then she thought, I know...I'll ask an angel for help, and surrounded herself with an egg-of-light.

She managed to read out the message! "I will help peace on Earth by looking after slugs."

She was ecstatic. She liked this angel thing.

Potty didn't seem very impressed with the content of her message, but thanked her for taking everyone else's messages. Then she explained that the whole school was going to help Torma by planting a thousand trees to offset the damage to the planet caused by her flights to reach Asia before she could start her hike.

Torma had never been so proud in her whole life. Afterwards, other kids came up and said nice things to her. At last, she thought, I feel better than them.

Fatch out! FangFang jumped into her mind suddenly. *Fat's your ego falking.*

"What's an ego?"

It's fat fart of you fich finks it fows all the answers.

Torma giggled. "Are you my ego, FangFang?"

Fo, invisible fide.

Did he mean died? Or fried? Or maybe hide... Ah, could be guide.

Invisible guide? Okay. She pressed him to tell her more, but he wouldn't. It was as though he'd told her too much already. This is going to get confusing, she thought. How do I know which voices in my head are guides, which are angels and which is my ego? Life was a lot easier when I just had playmates. I know – from now on, I'm only going to listen to FangFang, no one else, not even angels. I always know when it's him. He's the foolish one!

There were other things to concentrate on – importantly to drag the aunts along to meet Tenzin in the market. She couldn't wait to tell him the good news about going to Tibet.

"Hey, Squirt that's amazing!" he said, completely gobsmacked. And then grinned from ear to ear. She'd never seen anyone so happy – except perhaps the green alien in the last film she'd watched, turning princesses into slugs. She thought, if I die tomorrow I'll know at least I've done one good deed in my life.

"I'll find the heart of your country and your sister's penguin," she told Tenzin.

Aunt Yuhu looked extremely doubtful and Aunt Ani put her arm around Torma saying, "Tibet's a big place, Torma." She ignored them. She was on a roll. After all, she'd achieved so many miracles to get this far; a few more wouldn't hurt. And anyway she had FangFang on her side...

Foolish!...

Tenzin told her all the information he could about the penguin. "We were about ten days' walk south of the west river and two weeks' walk from the Nepalese border, Squirt. But we were nomads." He shrugged. "It's not much to go on. On the positive side, it's probably the only pint-sized penguin in Tibet!" She caught the twinkle in his eye, suddenly realising the impossibleness of the task of going on a wild penguin chase, and collapsed into hopeless giggles.

She didn't notice the shadow that skitted across his face as she turned to go.

On the way back she skipped along the pavement in front doing somersaults over roadwork barriers that landed her feet in fresh concrete. A cross road-man shooed her off. What's his problem? she thought. I can't see a 'No somersaulting' sign…

"Slow down! Wait for us!" Aunt Yuhu shouted. "We certainly won't have to wait for you when hiking. I needn't have worried about you not having time to train like we did, walking long days and climbing up hills." It didn't bother Torma. Training sounded boring. If Tenzin could do it, then she could, too. Anyway, she was always waiting for the aunts, they were so slow, and they had explained they were going to have animals to help carry stuff, so help would be at hand if need be.

But there was one exercise she couldn't get out of. Granny sat her down one day looking serious so she did her best to concentrate, though she was so excited wondering what it would be like walking along with animals she couldn't sit still. "Torma-la, there's something really important I want you to do for me."

"Anything, Granny."

"You know we try and keep the old Tibetan ways alive… Well, If I was younger I'd give anything to come with you and do a proper pilgrimage by walking along doing prostrations."

"What are prostrations?"

Granny stood up, put her hands together in the air, on her mouth, and on her heart and then bent stiffly down to put hands on the carpet and slide forward until she was lying flat out, forehead down. Then she slowly raised her hands up and down, bent back onto her heels, stood up and placed hands on heart again. "That's a prostration. And you need to say the correct words as you do it."

"Oh my goodness. You looked like a slug!"

From Granny's expression, those weren't the words...

"Say, 'I bring peace with my actions, my words and my thoughts,'" she said. "And imagine something pure like the sun... It's a way of honouring the land and the Tibetan way. D'you think you can do it?"

"Of course!"

She tried it out.

"I'm a lot quicker than you, Granny, but I'll do it for you. It'll be like bringing some of you with me."

They hugged each other hard and cried a bit.

The time was getting close. They were almost packed when a note and a parcel arrived from Tenzin. The note was addressed to Aunt Ani and Aunt Yuhu, but Granny opened it by mistake without thinking. She read it and sat down, suddenly turning very pale. Torma grabbed the note to see what it said.

Dear Ani-la and Yuhu-la
I don't wish to alarm you but I ought to let you know I think I am being followed.

You will understand I cannot say who by. It has been more apparent since I told Torma-la that I'd witnessed something bad during my escape. So she may be being watched too. Please look after her. She is precious to me.

Tashi delek

Tenzin

Torma had skimmed the first part without taking anything in, but was delighted to read, 'Please look after her. She is precious to me.' It made her feel special, and even more excited. She stuffed the note into her pocket, where it was forgotten.

"Look, Granny. He's sent me a parcel!"

It was beautifully wrapped in a red Tibetan bag, with a note saying, 'Good luck, Squirt. These are to help you find all the strength you need.' She eagerly untied the ribbon and opened it. Out popped three little black-and-white soft-toy penguins. Yay! Perfect! She was sure having them would help her find the lost penguin. Cuddling her new friends, she turned to Granny, who was trying bravely to keep smiling by busying herself with the luggage.

"What shall we call them?"

"Well, my sweet girl, they look like peace penguins to me. It'll help you remember the prostration words if you call them Act Peace,

Speak Peace and Think Peace."

And so it was decided. They were given harnesses made of hair-ties and attached to Torma's shiny new rucksack.

She was ready for the adventure.

If she had known then what was to come, she would never have walked out the front door.

ANGELIC REALM

9

Watch Out!

"This is FangFang reporting for lessons!" the new apprentice said happily. He was beginning to get used to the name. It made him feel strong and fierce. More in control of things. He rather liked that.

"Don't get too cocky," said Honey Angel. "Now *your* ego's talking. It spoils your vibes."

"Janglin' angels! he retorted. "It's impossible to get my vibes right all the time…"

"Of course, but the more you practise the better it gets. And the more you can help our girl. Keep that in mind. And remember the bigger picture of what we're doing is to help Earth and all beings. It'll keep you going when things get tricky."

"Uh-oh!…"

"Now, what did you notice when we told our girl about her ego?

"That she thought it was funny I called her a fat fart."

"That wasn't exactly the observation I had in mind… What about her vibe-catcher?"

"Dunno… Uh-oh!…"

"Oh dear… Do look at the light she's giving out… When the ego was in control her vibe-catcher went dull…the clues are there. Try and look for the light being given out when loving actions are happening, like giving hugs or prostrations being done."

"I will try harder…"

"Well done… You're doing brilliantly… See what a difference it made pointing out the angels when our girl put light around herself. That changed her life. Most humans go through their lives wishing they could see angels and never do.

"And she's setting off on an adventure without

her granny, but knowing she has a FangFang friend with her... That'll give her confidence. I'm afraid she's going to need it."

EARTH REALM

10

The Himalayas

Torma watched out of the window of the plane as the dying sun set the sky on fire, chased by a brand-new moon. She was transfixed. She'd never flown before. She felt as though she was an angel – wings outstretched. She was surprised to see the Earth as one entity, rather than a muddle of different countries all trying to be important, which was the impression she'd always got from grown-ups.

The moon seemed so close. It became darker outside and she idly reached up to try to touch it through the plastic of the window, as though she could catch a moonbeam.

As she did this the cabin lights of the plane went on. This spoiled the magic. Now all she could see was her reflection and what was going on behind her. She didn't like what she saw. A man was standing in the aisle staring at her. He was dressed all in black – black jacket, black sunglasses, even a black trilby hat, like the sort that dogs eat in films when they're trying to tear someone apart. It made her shiver. She didn't dare turn round until Aunt Ani returned from the washroom, squeezing through to the seat beside her. Closely followed by Aunt Yuhu in a tizzy about the lack of rice on the dinner menu.

"That geezer in black gives me the creeps," she told Aunt Ani.

"What geezer?" Aunt Ani asked, looking round.

The Geezer-in-Black had gone.

"Try and get some sleep," Aunt Ani coaxed. So Torma curled up with her three soft-toy penguins, working out which was which. Act Peace was fatter, Speak Peace had a bigger beak and Think Peace had eyes that were nearly closed. She loved them. They made her feel close to Tenzin.

She wanted to be courageous like him more than anything. But the flight became long and boring. She missed FangFang who was strangely not around.

Then in the middle of the night the plane landed in a hot country surrounded by desert, where men walked around in white sheets and ladies covered their faces up. They had to wait for hours at the airport for another plane. Aunt Ani, desperate for a cup of coffee, wasn't happy until a kind cleaning man bought her one.

"What can I give you?" she asked him.

"You can pray for me," he said.

"Ah, now there's a good international currency," said Aunt Yuhu. "Let's pay for things in prayers. I like it."

"In that case we're pingpong rich," said Aunt Ani. "The thousand peace messages that we're carrying are all like prayers."

Torma was more interested in some huge bronze sculptures she found to climb on.

It wasn't until they were clambering wearily up the steps into their second plane that she looked back at the other passengers and noticed the Geezer-in-Black walking across the tarmac behind them. He seemed to pull his hat down over his face as she looked at him and this made her feel uncomfortable. She hurried into the plane behind her aunts, and was distracted by Aunt

Yuhu fussing.

"Where are we going to wee in Tibet? I'm told there'll be no trees and sometimes no rocks to go behind... I wish I'd brought a big umbrella as recommended... I'm just going to have to hide behind a yak..."

Torma missed FangFang even more. Grown-ups can be so boring.

The day went very quickly, heading due east over the Earth, catching up time. Torma was dozing when she was woken gently with "Wake up! Look...out the window..." The sky was on fire again and the new moon back in position. But this time beneath it was an unbelievable sight. Stretching as far as she could see were snow-capped mountains reaching up above the endless sea of red-tinted clouds. It was an entire line, west to east, of magnificent white peaks of all sizes. Like an immense barrier placed there to guard something precious beyond.

Torma stared in awe. "We're going to walk across that?" she asked, wide-eyed.

Aunt Ani nodded. "Yes, the Himalayas. The greatest range on Earth."

Was it possible?

ANGELIC REALM

11

Jellyfish

Meanwhile there was a problem in the Angelic realm. FangFang was agitated.

"Honey, Why can't I get through to our girl? She can't hear me. Jumpin' jellyfish! I'm doing the egg bit…but she's missing out some of Earth time and I can't seem to keep up with that… Jumpin' jellyfish! What's happening?"

"Calm down! All's well. Yup, plane travel can cause imbalances in the vibes of humans as the pressures are so intense. You just have to work on getting back in tune with her…"

FangFang tried to see himself floating on the sea… He was in the water, but being bombarded by wriggly green jellyfish with long, tangly tentacles, jumping all over him like gooey wobbly slime… Jumpin' jellyfish!!

"See what you're making happen," Honey Angel laughed… "First get yourself steady… Then focus on something that's easy to see…like the peace messages that the humans carry… See the bright light coming from them… This is the light that we angels can put to use for good purposes."

FangFang managed to see the light and calm himself down. Well, more or less…

"The Peace Angels are very excited to have these messages." Honey continued, "When they're spoken out from sacred high places it multiplies the light the angels can use. There'll be great celebration. So many places on Earth are in need of peace at the moment. We need as many positive human vibes as we can get. Many of the angels with different jobs, like the Healing Angels or the Joy Angels, are calling for more light and love from the Earth Realm so that they can fulfil all the work that is being asked of them."

"Uh-oh!… Why can't you use your light?"

"'Cos it needs low vibes to fix Earth Realm problems. Using high vibes can over-energise and blow things sky-high if we're not careful."

"Like our girl can hear me but not you? So you need my low-vibe energy?"

"Exactly…though many humans don't hear these calls," she mumbled sadly.

"Uh-oh!…" said FangFang. "I'd like to be of help…that is if I'm ever reconnected." It was this thought of wanting to be there that seemed to whoosh him back down through the shift tunnel to the Earth Realm, light as a feather – no problem at all.

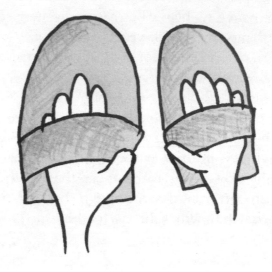

EARTH REALM

12

The Chonkas

"Yay! The fabled city of Kathmandu," said Torma, still excitedly nose-glued to the window of the plane as they twisted down between mountains and bumped heavily onto the short runway. They were at one and a half thousand metres above sea-level in the alluring Himalayan country of Nepal.

The airport was chaotic and noisy, smelling of

stale sweat and spicy incense. Torma held tight to Aunt Ani's hand until they were reunited with their luggage and had escaped the inside crush for the smog-ridden one outside. There they bounced off in a rattly old taxi enveloped by a cloud of dust.

Torma was used to city-living, but had trouble trying to take in the mess she was seeing here. *Real* mess – unlike Granny's description of her room at home. Buildings were falling to bits. Drivers were shouting. And with so many people in the road it took ages to jostle along around potholes, scooters carrying whole families, electric wires flapping dangerously and sickly dogs.

A hungry-looking woman clutching a baby banged on the window hoping for money as they turned into a narrow street with bright clothes stalls.

"Aunt Yuhu, why does everyone look so poor?"

"There was a big earthquake here recently, Torma-la. It brought down buildings and many people died. And they just don't have the money to put everything back together."

Torma looked up at a crumbling pile of faded bricks which, according to a sign, had once been a school, and shivered, moving closer to Aunt Yuhu. That was when she heard in her mind:

The people here are rich.

"FangFang! You're here!!" she exclaimed excitedly.

"Pardon?" said Aunt Yuhu.

"No, nothing," said Torma. She didn't realise she'd spoken out loud. She'd have to be more careful when talking to FangFang.

"FangFang I thought you'd gone. I've missed you. Where've you been?" she said in her mind.

Trying to keep up with you flying on a plane. My wings were being serviced!

"Idiot!"

At least I don't have to worry about wrecking the Earth by using a plane!

"Well... I'm going to help my school plant a thousand trees when I get back. We're going to raise lots of money for it. We'll feel rich. But I can't see how the people here are rich. Looks to me like no one has enough to eat."

I can see the vibes they give out. Richness is found in the heart.

Torma watched a skinny old cow pooing in the middle of the road and a woman rushing through the traffic to collect the poo in the folds of her dress. This caused swerving and honking and an old guy almost fell off his bicycle, but everyone seemed to make way for her, accepting this was how the day was...

"FangFang, that's gross!! If that woman's so rich why's she picking up cow poo?"

FangFang chuckled.

She had difficulty understanding this richness

thing. Even Aunt Ani had said richness is having peace messages.

They checked into a tall, thin hotel, with food not unlike that at home – minus the slugs. And, in the morning, set off on a mission. "I promised Granny we'd find you some chonkas, Torma-la," said Aunt Ani, "So we have to do this before we leave Kathmandu tomorrow."

"What're chonkas?"

"They're sort of gloves made of very hard wood, that slide along the ground when doing the prostrations that Granny taught you. Tibetans have always used them."

They toured the city in another rickety taxi...but no one could sell them any chonkas. Eventually they ended up at a massive temple known as a stupa, festooned with colourful flags. There were stalls all around selling Tibetan things, which reminded Torma of Tenzin's London stall. But even here no one had chonkas.

They were about to give up and head back to the hotel when an old Tibetan monk in dusty maroon robes approached them. Aunt Ani placed her hands together on her heart in the typical Himalayan greeting, saying "Namaste!" – meaning 'Hello to the good in you!' – and reached for her purse to give him some money, but the monk held up a gnarled hand to stop her. "Namaste! No, I was wandering how I could help *you*," he said.

"We're looking for some chonkas for a sacred journey to the magic mountain," explained Aunt Ani. The old monk beamed with delight. "I've been expecting you," he said. "Wait here." With that he scuttled off like a beetle in a race.

They waited patiently in the hot sun until they heard the scratching of floppy sandals scuttling back to them. He looked overjoyed. In his hands were two pieces of beautifully polished sandalwood with denim-blue canvas straps which he offered to Torma. "Here. Chonkas." She wasn't sure how they worked but felt the importance of them and smiled gratefully at the old monk.

"From the chief monk at my monastery," he said. "They're his most precious possessions, so have to be treated with great respect. He's used them to do prostrations for sixty years. He's always wanted to take them to the magic mountain, but has never been allowed back into Tibet. Now he gives them to you."

As the aunts chatted to the old monk, Torma wondered, why do people here give away their most precious possessions? And how did the old monk know they were coming?

It's the magic which Tibetans live by, came in FangFang. You'll be part of it by doing the prostrations. I can see how it works from the vibes. Go on. Try it with the chonkas.

Torma put a hand through each canvas strap and

practised swimming through the air with them.

FangFang giggled. You look like you've got flippers!

"Be serious, FangFang. Help me. I want to get it right and find out about this Tibetan magic."

Okay. Get out your three little penguins...

"FangFang..."

I'm being serious. This'll help!

"Okay." Torma walked over to a low wall around the temple and lined them up, watched by a tiny barefoot-girl in a pink dress.

Now what did Granny say you had to name them?

"Act Peace, Speak Peace and Think Peace."

Okay. You have to concentrate on each one as you do the movements. First clap your chonkas above your head and think, 'I bring peace with my actions.'

She banged the wood together loudly above her head. It made an echoing sound.

Next clap them in front of your mouth and think, 'I bring peace with my words.'

This made Torma giggle.

Now clap in front of your heart and think, 'I bring peace with my thoughts.'

"But my thoughts come from my head."

No they don't.

"Yes they do."

Anyway, then you do the prostration.

As she lay down with her hands in the chonkas in front of her and touched her head to the ground, remembering how Granny had done it, from the corner of her eye she spotted the tiny barefoot-girl grabbing the three penguins with one swift movement and running off as fast as her little legs could manage.

It took Torma a few seconds to realise what was happening. "Oy! Those are my peace penguins!" She jumped up, threw down the chonkas and chased the tiny girl, grabbing the penguins back. Then holding them tightly, laughing with the tiny girl, she ran on round the circular wall, until bumping, bang, straight into a man in black. There was a nasty smell.

Oh no... It was the Geezer-in-Black from the plane.

He grabbed her and she screamed. This seemed to make him hold her tighter. She stamped down hard on the top of his foot. He yelled in pain and released his grip just enough for her to wriggle free and run on round the temple, searching for the aunts.

When she found them, she burst into fearful tears.

"Whatever's the matter?"

"Doing prostrations is meant to be in a state of peace, Torma-la."

"Where are the chonkas?"

All she could do was sob, uncontrollably.

"Oh no! We had to treat them with utmost respect and somehow you've managed to lose them already."

They searched for over an hour, but there was no sign of them.

"C'm on. We'll go back to the hotel… We have to get ready for the journey tomorrow."

That night Torma lay on her bed unable to sleep, crying fitfully. "FangFang, why do I always get so scared?"

It's all part of life's richness through which we learn and grow.

"Nonsense. I don't want any more richness."

She didn't feel the Hugging Angel he managed to send. She just pictured the face of the Geezer-in-Black looming over her.

Why was he there? Could he be an Invader?

ANGELIC REALM

13

Eggs for Homework

Meanwhile, FangFang was pleased with himself.
"Hey I've lost the f letter lisp. Coolish! Our girl
can understand me better now."

"Well done," said Honey Angel. "You're seeing
what she needs, so becoming more in tune with
her. And you're laughing together. That makes for
good friends."

"But when she's scared she won't listen to me."

"Yup, fear puts up walls. But you'll find it easier to connect when higher in the mountains. The screen between the Angelic and Earth Realms is thinner there."

"Coolish!"

"Remember to use the egg-of-light for her as well as yourself. The more love there is the more everything flows happily. Encourage her to think positively and understand that she's safe and can always ask for help. Though remember, angels can't help unless asked."

"Uh-oh!... But why?"

"'Cos to ask an angel for help opens the door to the heart."

"Okay. So can angels change human vibe-catchers?"

"No, humans have to do that for themselves."

"But Honey did you see the vibe-catcher of the woman who'd picked up the cow poo? It was shining with joy."

"Yup, well spotted. She now had fuel with which to cook her children a meal. There was such love for them," said Honey Angel. "And if you look round Kathmandu you'll see that the vibe-catchers are bigger and brighter than in many cities of the world...and what's more important they reach out and touch others. There's not that sense of separation that so many other cities have.

Here everyone lives more together and isn't afraid to share the same space."

"Coolish! Like when they say 'Namaste... Hello to the good in you', and their vibe-catchers are shining?"

"Exactly. It's a way for hearts to touch each other – often those of total strangers. There's a lovely acceptance of other people's beliefs here which enables the physical poverty to bring richness to the heart – as you so rightly told our girl. C'mon. Let's tumble-rumble and see if she's cheering up."

"Jumpin' jellyfish! It's eggs for homework..." sang FangFang.

EARTH REALM

14

Vomit

"I'm sorry, I didn't mean to lose the chonkas," Torma apologised to Aunt Ani the next morning. She was still feeling cross with herself about it.

"Well, all things have their purpose. We must trust it's meant to be this way. It'll mean the prostrations will be hard on your hands, but sadly we can't search any more. We have to catch the local plane. We're going by Yeti Airlines."

After a delay of six hours at the airport, Aunt Yuhu, pacing up and down with rice-withdrawal symptoms, had renamed it "Not Yeti Airlines". Torma didn't mind the waiting. She felt this whole long journey to reach the high mountains was somehow part of the adventure, like the anticipation of waiting for a birthday. Anyway she had a good yeti book to read. She'd read other stories about this ancient beast that roamed the Himalayas, so was wildly excited they were finally heading into the land of the yeti. It gave her so many questions. Would they see him? What did he look like? Was he aggressive…? She knew a lot of people thought the yeti was only a myth. Adults always need proof of things. What do *they* know about it? She was sure FangFang would agree. He always understood. Though there was no sign of him. Sometimes he was as illusive as the yeti. No doubt having trouble with planes again.

The flight took them west to a town in the lowlands, to a hotel where she couldn't work out if the en-suite was a toilet or a shower, and they found another flight on a tiny plane the following morning. This one only had room for a few passengers and not much luggage. By now Torma had a churning stomach. She was feeling too sick to care about anything. She couldn't even have tackled ice cream. She lay her head against the window on her friends, the three precious soft penguins, eyes closed, and hoped they'd get there quickly.

The plane made so much noise she could barely hear Aunt Ani shouting, "Wow! Look at the mountains," and "That must be our pingpong river – it's beautiful." But the little plane was tossing and turning in the air currents, making her feel worse still. And now FangFang was trying to come in and tell her something, but she wasn't in the mood for talking. "Go away FangFang. I think I'm going to vomit."

She wasn't sure if she was dreaming or not when she saw a picture of Tenzin in her mind. He was smiling at her and looking hopeful. It was a reminder of her promise to him – to find the heart of Tibet and the lost penguin. This made her feel stronger. And finally she opened her eyes as Aunt Ani shook her and yelled, "We're coming up to land. How 'bout that! The plane's coming *up* to land!"

Through the grubby and scratched windows Torma could see they were floating steeply up like a bird of prey, wings alarmingly close to wooded mountain slopes, heading for a wide, flat ledge on a cliff top, with more mountains beyond. She gasped fearfully. It looked like they were heading straight into the cliff, and the little plane was labouring as though puffing and panting hard. She willed it to rise up. Strangely, this new strength in her brought about by the promise, was making a difference. "You can do it! C'mon!" She held her breath.

It wasn't until she saw grass beneath her – so close she could have counted the blades – that she realised they'd come over the cliff edge. She breathed out a sigh of relief. They bumped down, swaying giddily, onto a small concrete landing strip. The brakes roared as the plane came to a stop.

As soon as steps were dragged to the door and it was creaked open – as though with a tin-opener – she flopped out and staggered to the edge of the strip, where there was a brown patch, and promptly vomited. The brown patch turned out to be a chicken laying an egg. It squawked off indignantly, none too delighted with the latest arrivals. Torma collapsed shakily on some grass, cuddling her penguins close, curling up into a ball, letting the bright sunshine caress her cheeks, now wet with tears. Soon the shaking stopped and she felt a bit better. I really hope no one saw me, she thought. But she could see the aunts deep in conversation and felt sure they'd be talking about how it'd been a mistake to bring her. Worse still, might they even send her home?

To distract herself she looked around. The landing strip was perched high on the ledge along with a small village. There were no roads, just ramshackle houses, made of loose stone with tin roofs. To the north there were snow-capped mountains. To the south the cliff, and a drop down to a deeply carved river, and beyond to more mountains. The sky dominated everything. But no ordinary sky. It was the clearest, brightest, sparkliest blue Torma had ever seen. It was as though they had risen above the mess that humans create and were now in a place good enough for angels.

Jumpin' jellyfish! Certain arrivals are making a mess here! came in FangFang.

This made Torma giggle, which made her feel better still. She allowed herself to be helped up by a young man in jeans and cap, who introduced himself as Jampa. "Namaste, hello to the good in you! Welcome to paradise. Rough flight up was it? You'll soon feel okay. Though we're at an altitude of three thousand metres here, so it'll take a day or two to get used to. I'll be guiding you, following the great river through the mountains to the Tibetan border with the mules." He surprisingly didn't look many years older than she was, and rather too thin and gentle to be a guide, but she looked into kind, smiley eyes that reflected the sky, and immediately felt warm and safe. Luckily he didn't seem remotely bothered by the way she'd messed up the chicken, saying, "She must have wanted to

welcome you with an egg. You must be special…
Good aim by the way! Don't worry. The dogs will
soon lick the vomit off."

Gross!

"Shut up, FangFang. I need to be on my best
behaviour."

She followed Jampa with two kit bags on his
shoulders, and a woman in a long, colourful skirt
with the other bag, leading them along a dusty
track between buildings to a substantial new one
with verandahs, where they would stay. A large
sheet was spread outside and smiley locals were
shaking sunflowers onto it to catch the seeds –
important food for protein. Torma longed to have
a go too.

But she was even more interested in the trail
which led off behind the house. Their route
tomorrow. She couldn't wait to meet the mules
and to set off on the hike, even though, for the
first time, she worried if she'd be able to keep up.

Course you will, said FangFang. I'll be with
you. Together we can take on the world!

How do you hug a voice in your head? Torma
wasn't quite sure, but tried to do it anyway.

That evening, just as shining pink clouds were
painting the sky, they had a ceremony to bless
their journey. Bit like the opening ceremony at the
Olympic Games, thought Torma, as she grabbed
the peace penguins and walked the short distance

with the dudey aunts to the centre of the village, where there was an open courtyard with a tall flagpole in the middle. Along one side was a small shed, filled by a huge gold and maroon prayer-wheel, which they spun around. It took quite an effort, as it was heavy. "It's filled with pingpong peace messages," explained Aunt Ani. "We're sending them out when we spin it round." Torma watched, mesmerised, wondering why some sort of magic was touching her heart.

Outside, they were met by an old woman dressed in what appeared to be tablecloths and large jewellery, who seemed to smile with her whole self. Her small grand-daughter, clung to her skirts, staring up with big, innocent eyes. Though the temperature was dropping rapidly and the wind icy, the small girl was dressed only in a t-shirt, and was shivering from the cold. They were keen to join the ceremony.

All through the lighting of candles and speaking of peace messages, the small girl stared at Torma, who wondered what it would be like to be her. It made her feel uncomfortable. Our lives are so different, thought Torma. I've got things like food and clothes and toys, which I'm sure she doesn't have. That made her feel guilty.

Go on! said FangFang.

"Go on what?"

You know...

"I can't, FangFang. They're an important gift from Tenzin. What would he say?"

He'd say, 'Squirt, you're so compassionate'.

Things were different in these mountains – more reckless...

15

Pride

"Hey, Honey!" FangFang said, proudly puffing himself up. "Janglin' angels! I'm getting good at this! Our girl's really listening to me and she gave me a mind hug…and did you see how well that picture worked to remind her about her promise and bring willpower?"

Honey Angel sighed. "Yes, that picture you

sent did help bring positive change. But I wasn't so impressed with your egg work…"

"How was I to know she'd vomit on the chicken?"

"Yup, well… Humans do funny things in the Earth Realm. You have to remember that your role as an invisible guide is about gently reminding her who she is – about the strength she has within herself. It's not about you. You have to learn to put yourself aside."

FangFang felt humbled. "Hmmm, maybe that's right. There are times when I feel that there's a memory of something I've experienced previously trying to come through, even though it's been erased… That's when I can't connect up properly…"

"Be peaceful within yourself and it'll all work."

"I really will try better, Honey. I can do this."

As she faded out he was sure he heard a faint whisper: "Pride comes before a fall…"

EARTH REALM

16

Careful What You Wish For

"I'm as excited as a slug in a rug," Torma was saying to FangFang.

She'd barely slept that night. But at last, as morning dawned, their hiking procession set off along the trail north. First went the mules – seven of them. Strapped precariously to their backs were the three kit bags containing their personal things and the all-important sleeping bags – nights were going to be very cold here – along with tents, mattresses, stoves, fuel, pots and pans and some basic foods like rice, flour and oil, which had been brought up on the plane. Vegetables and potatoes had been acquired in the village. Ice cream was off the menu!

Three men, the muleteers, followed, brandishing sticks to tap the mules along from time to time when they stopped for too long to nibble grass. Then came a cook, who strode along swinging a tall pile of egg-boxes tied up with string. And the smiley-eyed guide, Jampa, who seemed to float effortlessly up the trail but stayed close to the dudey aunts, in pink and blue hats, singing and chanting happily as they plodded with heavy steps, swinging their walking poles.

Finally, Torma brought up the rear, managing to ignore her pink jacket and feeling thrilled to be part of this great adventure. Aunt Yuhu had insisted she wear a sun hat, thankfully not pink, and sunglasses, which made her feel foolish, but she proudly carried her rucksack holding waterproofs, water bottle, apple and book. Strapped to the back were two peace penguins, Speak Peace and Think Peace.

She also carried in her mind the picture of a

small girl smiling from ear to ear, cuddling Act Peace tightly. This made her heart feel as light as a feather.

The mission bit isn't going that well so far, she thought. No sign of the lost penguin and I'm now one more penguin down.

The trail followed along the high slopes of the river valley, which had been deeply carved out aeons ago. It was stony and rough and not always easy to negotiate. But Torma skipped along happily, feeling like a bird in the sky as she peered steeply down to the great river far below. It seemed to call to her. She wished she could reach out and touch it. At first there were houses near the village with people going about their work, gathering produce from the little terraced fields clinging to the precipitous sides, or tending goats and sheep.

"Everyone's preparing themselves for winter," said Jampa. "There's six months of heavy snow when we barely go outside and so have to gather enough food and wood for the fires to feed our families, and also our animals, who live on the ground floor of our houses. This helps to keep us warm."

Uh-oh!... Sounds a bit smelly! said FangFang.

"Shush! FangFang. Don't be annoying. I'm trying to listen."

"It's all about survival," continued Jampa. "We've lived like this for generations – in harmony with Nature. Our people are the same as the Tibetans over the border. All part of the same land. We're a very long way from what people in the cities call civilisation. We rely on each other. We can't depend on anybody elsewhere for anything."

The trail meandered on, climbing steadily upwards, gradually leaving any signs of human habitation behind, except for a cluster of huts at the top of a ridge, where three great eagles circled majestically above them. It made Torma feel vulnerable. A feeling which became stronger as the trail continued downwards for a while into a dark pine forest. She kept herself close to Jampa and asked, "What about the wild animals? How do they survive the winter?"

"Like us all. They just have to find what they can. We get little musk deer and black bear – one killed a cow the other day – and golden jackal. You'll probably hear them howling tonight...and away from the trail there's striped hyena and sometimes mountain tiger, though even he's not as secretive as the snow leopard."

"And yeti?" asked Torma, suddenly remembering the advice that Granny always gave. That if you needed to escape from a yeti you had to run downhill so his shaggy long hair would get in his eyes and obstruct his vision...

"Yes, and yeti," said Jampa, eyes smiling even

more than usual.

Torma grinned and said to FangFang inwardly, "Wouldn't it be cool to return to school and tell the other kids I've seen yetis?"

This seemed to make FangFang unusually quiet, as though he was working something through. Eventually he said:

I'm told we have to be careful what we wish for.

"You're no fun," she said. "That's just dumb."

She turned to chat with the dudey aunts instead. They were concentrating on leaving the magic crystals along the way. Aunt Ani explained to Torma, "Here, take one and see if there's a spot which feels right to place it. Then hide it there." Torma hid the crystal at the base of a beautiful rock where a lizard scurried by. He stopped mid-scurry and looked up at Torma with large piercing eyes as if to say 'Never fear, I will be the guardian of this crystal. We all work together here...'

Aunt Ani then taught her a few specific words – a mantra – to repeat, saying "You mustn't tell anybody what the mantra is. It's for this special journey to connect us up with the natural systems all around. So you'll be in tune with the nature fairies."

Torma nodded fiercely. She wasn't sure she could keep it secret from FangFang. But he was being so boring she didn't care. She found it so intriguing that it affected her physically. She could feel the excitement climbing up the back of her neck.

"Like a magic spell?" she asked Aunt Ani, with big round lizard eyes.

"Yes," Aunt Ani replied, smiling and giving her a cuddle. "With our crystal placements we're creating a river of silver light which is side-by-side with the great river down there, leading us all the way to the magic mountain. This will open up an energy door, a portal, for light to enter to help the pingpong planet."

"Although," sighed Aunt Yuhu, leaning heavily on her poles, "we really need to physically connect up more with the great river. It'd make the work more effective. Sadly I don't think the trail goes down close for a couple of days. I tried throwing a crystal at it but it's too far away."

Torma thought she looked tired.

After a further couple of hours, when she rounded a bend and saw Aunt Ani agitated and Aunt Yuhu sitting flopped on the ground with her boot off, she wondered how she could help. "It's only a blister," Aunt Yuhu was saying.

Jampa took charge. "We'll wait here for a bit while you rest and recover. First I'm just going to run ahead to tell the muleteers to make camp up ahead," and he dashed off. Aunt Ani dug around in her rucksack for pills and plasters.

It was at this point that Torma noticed a narrow, overgrown track which seemed to head from the main trail straight down to the river. A seed of an idea sprouted. What if…what if I sprinted down while the aunts are waiting here and I brought back some of the river to them? Then they'd be able to connect up with it properly. They'd be so pleased with me. And I'd be playing my part to help.

She investigated. It looked like a bit of pushing through vegetation, but with lots of roots and branches to hold onto where it got steep. Before she knew it she was heading down the track. She thought she heard someone calling, but by then she was committed. Anyway she'd be back really quickly. Then the track seemed to turn more into a stream and became so muddy she was slipping and sliding down on her bottom. She thought she heard in her mind, Remember you've got to climb back up, but took no notice. She was still cross with FangFang.

Anyway, now she could hear the river. How exciting! It became louder and louder – a great roar, almost. And suddenly she was there. She felt first the cold wind which was whooshing along above the rushing water. Then she saw it. Deep, turquoise blue. Lumps of glacial ice. White spray foaming. Torma held her breath in awe. It was some powerful river all right.

Okay! Concentrate. How to get down to it to collect the water? She was perched high on the bank – here, steeply sloping rock. She'd have to go along a bit. She took her rucksack off to take out the empty water bottle and started pushing her way through the undergrowth to the side. Sharp prickles snatched at her face and hands. Ouch!

The only clear space was close to the sloping rock at the water's edge. She crept down cautiously, carefully placing her boots on jutting-out rocks, and holding onto the vegetation with her free hand to steady herself. Then the footholds became a bit sparse, so she made a grab for a swaying branch above her head, just as her foot slipped. The branch came away in her hand. Just for a second she seemed to be held in space. Then she was falling. Oh poo!

Splash! A deep cold enveloped her with a thousand icy knives, forcing her to hold her breath. She floundered, kicking instinctively. Her head came to the surface. Gasping…gasping, while ice churned all around her. She was being carried down-river at a terrifying rate. Her feet and hands quickly went numb. She kicked harder, but waterlogged boots dragged her downwards and suddenly she was somersaulting over and over, and beginning to lose feeling in her face as well. It was then she thought she heard a shout above the din of the water and realised she was close to a rocky shore where a figure was standing. She kicked with all her might, willing herself forward, the same as when the plane had needed her – but now she needed the willpower herself. She had a promise to fulfil. I *have* to get there. I *can* do this. She reached an arm up above her head and suddenly a strong hand grabbed hers in a vice-like grip and she was hauled up into the air, dripping heavily and thrust uncomfortably onto a large, flat rock.

Phew!

Her hat and sunglasses had gone. The bottle had gone. She was frozen almost to the core. But she was alive! She spluttered and coughed and then looked gratefully up to her rescuer…to see a pair of dark, smouldering eyes underneath a black hat and nasty garlic breath. In that moment of recognition, she screamed as loud as she could.

It was the Geezer-in-Black.

ANGELIC REALM

17

Doubts

"Honey! Honey! Help! Please help! I've messed up. I've really messed up. I could've stopped her going down to the river." FangFang was frantic. "But I couldn't get through…"

It seemed to him that Honey was just a little reluctant to explain things. "Listen in to yourself… Be peaceful…use an egg-of-light…

And remember she needs to ask for help to open the energy before we angels can come in."

"I know, but..."

"She'll listen to you if you're calm. Believe in yourself more. Trust your own judgement. That way you'll grow. You know the answers yourself. You can do it."

"But you'll always be around, won't you Honey?" FangFang asked, anxiously.

"Yup, while I'm needed," Honey replied. "But when the time comes and you need to access information, if it's for good purpose, you can go to the great library where the 'book of life' is stored. All the records of everything that has ever happened, including the intention behind every action, is held here. Nothing is ever lost."

"How do I get there?"

"Same as everything else – you just imagine it strongly, and you'll be there.

They both heard it then – a call...urgent screams...

EARTH REALM

18

Out of the Frying-pan

"So, you leettle rat! What you doing een ze reever? Lucky I find you. Lucky for *me*, zat ees. You won't get away *zees* time. When I feeneesh weez you, you weell weesh you *had* drowned."

The Geezer-in-Black hauled Torma roughly up by the wrist. She had no problem understanding his English, spoken with a heavy Invader accent.

He handed her over to one of his men, who'd come up behind. "Look what we caught! Tie her up and gag her…and take her back to ze camp… Zees ees good news. It geeve me honour. And weell save us beeg effort – all zat following and watching. Zees calls for serious celebration."

"I haven't done anything!" screamed Torma. "Lemme go!" But she found herself with a scarf tied painfully tight around her mouth. Still, she struggled and kicked until the man swiped her across the face with the back of his hand. The ring he wore tore sharply into her cheek, forcing her into a stunned stillness. She was shivering violently, but didn't feel the cold. She had blood running down her face but didn't feel the pain; only an icy bubble of shock, licked by flames of fury. She started kicking and punching again.

"Quite a little fighter, ain' we?" The man took off his belt with one hand and, forcing her to the ground with a heavy boot, used it to tie her hands behind her back. He then picked her up and threw her, still kicking, over his shoulder, carrying her, scraping through spiny undergrowth, away from the rocks and noise of the river. Till they came shuffling into a clearing with a make-shift camp of four tents. A handful of men were sitting drinking around a fire.

Torma stopped kicking and listened. It sounded like the men were laughing uproariously at the man who was carrying her.

"Eh! Lost our trousers, 'ave we?"

"Eh! look at those knees, will ya!"

Even the Geezer-in-Black was there laughing. "When you dressed, tie our prize up een ze store tent and come and drink."

It was only when she'd been dumped unceremoniously in the corner of a tent, and tied to a heavy log, that she realised what'd been happening. The man had his trousers down around his ankles! He looked ridiculous. This was definitely the most trouble she'd ever been in but, muffled as she was through the tight scarf, she giggled.

It was the giggle that made the man turn around as he was leaving the tent, and something about what he saw softened him just enough to come back and untie the scarf around her mouth, saying, "I'll get it in the neck for this, so keep quiet…" And rushed out of the tent, pulling his trousers up as he went."

Torma took a deep breath. What to do? In all the books she'd read, people who were captured and tied-up always managed to escape. So of course she'd have to escape. But how to do it? FangFang would be no help. She'd been rude to him and he'd obviously left her. The dudey aunts had no idea where she was. Jampa had said, "We're a long way from civilisation. We can't depend on anyone else for anything." So that was it then. She'd have to do it herself.

She could hear the men getting drunk and laughing raucously. Someone would be bound to come in soon for more drink, which was stacked in one corner of the tent, so she'd have to be quick. She had to release her arms tied behind her back to the log. Yanking against it as hard as she could, she felt something in the ties give way and stretch enough for her to be able roll onto her side, then, with much wriggling, force her body one leg at a time back through her arms, till they were in front of her. An adult would not have been this flexible, but she was a supple child... Then it was for her teeth to set to work on the knot of the soft leather. In five minutes she had it loosened and prised open. By this time her wrists were red and raw. But she was free.

Quickly, she slipped out underneath the back of the tent and was able to dash across to the next one. She waited there to catch her breath. Was there a safe way to go without being spotted? She had to move, though her whole body was shaking with fear. But suddenly she realised she could hear the men clearly from here. They were still speaking English, presumably their common language, so she couldn't ignore what they were saying...

One man was sneering, "When we signed up

to come from our country to work for you we didn't know it'd be a pathetic assignment to watch a child."

The voice of the Geezer-in-Black was distinct in reply. "All right, we caught her now so I explain, 'cos eet's eemportant you understand. But eef one word of zees goes beyond us, I'll personally sleet all your zroats."

The men went silent. They were frightened of the Geezer-in-Black. With good reason...

"We watch her 'cos we believe she been sent to search for eenformation by London Tibetan who saw cheeldren being silenced before he escape Tibet. Zey were too close to secret nuclear missile site. Zat ees all I say about eet."

Torma gasped – and grabbed her mouth with her hand, hoping nobody'd heard. So that was what Tenzin hadn't wanted to tell her... No wonder.

"Eet took time to track heem down, after ze spy saw heem escape, but I'm sure he never said what he saw. Tibetans always know ze lives of zeir families are at risk eef zey open zeir mouss. Many years my London team been watching heem, along wiz ozer...creemeenals. And zen we heard heem geeving zees child directions, so zat must be why she eez here. Zough een my experience cheeldren can't be trusted 'cos zey're no good at being zreatened. Zey do what zey want not what's good for zem."

Torma wanted to shout, "Tenzin never told me about the children!" And "Those were directions to find the penguin!" but held her hand tight over her mouth.

"We cannot allow zees girl to speak and let ze eenformation out – no matter ze cost. Ozer countries must not know, or mine weell lose face – and beellions een trade. We already zreatened ze Tibetan, but we can't risk more weez him – he's protected by ze law een England... Ze Eentelleegence Bureau made eet very clear: trade ees too eemportant to risk an eenternational eenceedent."

Her eyes were wide with fear as he continued...

"Ze Bureau order me to capture ze child hush-hush, so no one knows she gone, and breeng her een alive for eenterrogation. Zen she weell be deesappeared – very easy een Tibet. So tomorrow we head for ze border. Tonight we celebrate zat our leettle rat has swum straight eento our hands!"

Torma froze. The Geezer-in-Black was definitely an Invader and the other men were working for him. There was no mistaking their intention. Every cell of her body seemed to fill with ice. She was done for. She couldn't possibly get out of this. A picture of Granny suddenly came into her mind – Granny who knew her sweet Torma would never come home. And her eyes filled with tears.

It was then that she heard him. It was FangFang

hissing in her mind.

Ask for help from the angels... Quick, ask for help.

But she was stuck. Not only was her body paralysed with fear, but her mind as well. It couldn't think.

It felt like FangFang was hitting it with a hammer...

C'MON!! Ask for help!

Still it was ice.

C'MON! You fan fo it. Ask for felp!

There was something about FangFang reverting to his f letter code which reached in and touched her ice-bound mind enough to create a small crack, which released a tiny "Help, please!"

Almost at that moment there was a disturbance on the far side of the clearing. An animal was struggling and thrashing noisily in a bush. Torma couldn't see it but realised that the men were distracted and the Geezer-in-Black was shouting, "Get zat damn deer before ze jackals pull eet to pieces. Eet's our deenner!!"

Torma breathed out and turned to escape in the opposite direction. But just then some familiar things caught her eye. Some things sticking out of a rucksack on a bedroll in the entrance to one of the other tents. It was the chonkas!

They were so close. But if she was spotted, she was the one who'd be dead meat. Did she dare risk getting them?

The deer squealed a high-pitched, terrified scream. There was a commotion going on.

Torma knelt down and wriggled on her tummy towards the bedroll. Then, making a lightning grab, and with barely a backwards glance at the struggle going on at the other end of the camp, she turned and ran. She ran as fast as she'd ever run. Swerving between trees. Through a tangled thicket and snatching spiky bushes. Tripping on jutting rocks. Across a large patch of squelchy yellow vegetation that threatened to suck her in. Heaving with all her might she made for harder ground that was covered in dense bushes. Pushing her way in she threw herself into a sandy hollow, curled herself up into a ball and covered her head with her arm. Panting hard.

After a couple of minutes she dared to lift her head and listen. All was quiet, except for the drumming of her wildly beating heart. "FangFang," she whispered in her mind. "Are you there?"

All was still quiet.

"FangFang, please be there. I really need you now. I'm so scared and all alone. I'm sorry. Please forgive me. FangFang, where are you? I think I'm going to cry."

She seemed to wait forever but a soft breeze enveloped her body like a hug and then she heard him.

Don't cry. It's okay. You'll get out of this. But you have to keep strong. You have all the strength you need inside. You have to keep going.

"But they'll see me."

You have to risk it. Go! Go uphill!

She kept to the thickest parts of the forest, where she wouldn't be seen from below, and started climbing. Using the chonkas on her hands in front of her face, she was able to push through dense bushes, and tried not to take any notice of all the cuts and bruises. She didn't dare stop again. Just briefly to listen for pursuers. But all seemed quiet. At least she had an aim now – to head uphill. She assumed that eventually she would meet the main trail. Though had no idea what to do then. At least it would give her options. If she missed the trail then the consequences were too dire to think about. And at least moving uphill kept her warm, for now she had time to realise that her clothes were still wet and it would soon be dark. She tried hard not to think of the dark.

After a while the forest changed to tall pine trees. This meant that the going was easier, but she felt vulnerable, as she could easily be spotted at a distance. When the pine forest floor became too steep she turned to follow a narrow ridge north for quite a way back into heavy scrub with mixed tree-cover. By now the sun had set and dusk was bringing a different sense – the scurrying and rustling of animal noises coming out for the nightshift. It was bringing the fear of the unseen. Her body became tense and her eyes alert, darting back and forth, unsure…

"FangFang, I'm so tired and hungry and thirsty. I have to find somewhere to sleep. Maybe there's a cave over there by those rocks? It's almost dark so it must be okay to stop." She made her way over to a rocky outcrop. She could dimly see an entrance of some sort in the rocks. Ah, it looked hopeful… But something didn't quite smell right.

Careful, cautioned FangFang.

Torma peered into the gloom between the rocks. Three pairs of eyes were staring back at her. She stood stock-still. She knew she was scared, but in a very detached sort of way. She felt a burst of energy and this wound her up ready for whatever was to happen, ready to spring like a wild animal. Suddenly there was a low growl. Then there were more growls. Then a snarl. She backed away very slowly indeed. And kept backing and backing. Three thin shapes appeared, like shadows, approaching her very slowly. Nothing was fast. She backed more and more. They advanced more and more. Out of the corner of her eye she could detect pine trees close by. Ones with good low branches to climb, she was almost sure. That remained to be seen. She would have to make a dash for it.

Go now!!! shouted FangFang.

She threw the chonkas at the shadows, which gave her the seconds she needed to swing herself frantically up into the branches of the nearest tree, thankfully old and gnarled, reassuringly sturdy. There was snarling. She smelt hot breath as things paced up and down beneath her.

What were they?

She tried to remember the animals that Jampa had spoken about. She was sure tigers didn't come in threes, and she would have been eaten pretty quickly had it been hungry tigers. Snow leopards were too rare and there wasn't enough snow here. Hyenas made a horrible laughing sound, she knew. Bears...well, maybe bears, but she thought you had to lie flat on the floor and play dead for a bear, and it was too late for that. Possibly yetis? But thrilling as that may be, she had a feeling they'd be bigger. Just then from across the darkened land came an eerie, screeching howl followed by yelps. And she remembered the jackals. Ah, that seemed the most likely.

She searched her memory for what she knew of jackals... Similar to wolves...mostly scavengers... hunt in packs...

But do jackals climb trees?

ANGELIC REALM

19

Life or Death

"Yup! you did it!" said Honey Angel. "Well done for sending the picture of Granny. That broke down the fear wall so she could hear you."

FangFang felt relieved. At least he'd got something right at last. "Coolish… And thank you for sending the deer, Honey. I saw shining light arrive immediately our girl asked for help."

"The sacrifice advanced the little deer's path. All beings are interrelated in the web of life."

"But that's death, not life…"

"Same thing. Death is an important part of life… His soul will have grown, giving him strength for the next challenge wherever that is. The chief angels might even ask him to go for training as an invisible guide… I hear it's quite a tough assignment…" Honey winked at FangFang. Angels don't often wink.

He felt all warm inside.

"Go on. Get back to work, before you start puffing up with pride again…"

EARTH REALM

20

Running Out of Time

"When we get home, I'm going to write a story called 'Sleeping in a tree was the most uncomfortable night ever...'"

That's the trouble with bodies...

"Idiot..." she murmured.

A soft glow was coming into the sky, spreading light over the tops of the mountains all around.

It was still bitterly cold in the forest, but the tree had given protection from the wind and the damp. And the nook that Torma had found, high up in the branches, was shaped like a hollow, which had stopped her falling out and given warmth on three sides.

"Thank you for being with me, FangFang. If it wasn't for you I think I would've died."

Not as bad as it sounds, said FangFang.

She didn't really take the comment on board. She was feeling pain in many parts of her body and gingerly touching the dried blood on her face, wondering what it looked like. Stretching her stiff limbs she pushed off the blanket of dried pine needles she'd buried herself in and peered downwards.

"Is anybody there?" she ventured.

Silence.

"I think they've gone." she said to FangFang

I wouldn't be too sure...

She watched patiently as the light slowly come down to the forest floor. Then detected a movement at the base of the tree. A flicker of an ear. Curled up in a tight ball against the trunk was something furry, sandy-brown flecked with grey, and a thin snout. It looked to be about the size of a collie dog.

"Morning Mr Jackal," she called quietly.

Both ears flickered. But he didn't move. She

looked around, but couldn't see anybody else. Which is not to say nobody else saw her. What should she do? Her lips were dry and cracked. Her throat was sore. And her tummy was very empty and rumbling. She would have given anything for a drink. But it didn't feel very safe to descend. Had the jackal just been having a sleep-over? Or was he hungry too?

Recite the magic mantra, came in FangFang.

"How d'you know about that? It's meant to be secret."

No secrets... I'm your guide... If you recite it you'll be in harmony with the natural systems...and the nature fairies.

"I'm never quite sure if I should listen to your ideas, FangFang...but here goes."

She recited the magic mantra over and over again. At first quietly and then gaining confidence till the sound was ringing through the trees. A butterfly flitted past. Numerous small birds appeared, twittering sweetly. Streams of sunlight poured down, picking up the brightest colours of the green leaves and a low bed of red raspberries. The jackal got up and lolloped quietly over to another tree, where he sat down again and gently watched her. Torma was sure he was smiling.

Feeling at ease she climbed carefully down and over to the raspberries. No breakfast had ever tasted so good. Overhead a brown-tipped bird of prey called and flew on up the valley side. Torma picked up her chonkas and followed that way. Climbing steadily, she pushed through the forest, looking behind her as she went. The jackal was coming too. Eventually she reached beyond the trees to where she could see the great river now shining far below, picking up the light. And to the south she could make out terraced farmland. Something seemed familiar.

Before long she came out onto a trail. This was definitely familiar. She could even see a place where a magic crystal had been left. She took the way north. After a while she turned and saw that the jackal, although still watching, wasn't going to follow.

"Bye! Mr Jackal," she called softly. "Thank you."

The sun was high overhead by the time she came to the place where she'd left the aunts yesterday and taken the route to the river. It seemed like a long time ago. Now the track looked well trampled, as though many people had been down it, with footprints in the dirt around where it joined the trail. Here was a large arrow, built from stones, pointing north. Following the direction along the trail, it wasn't long before she heard voices and came down to a little grassy terrace holding three red tents. She could see people, one in a pink hat. Cooking smells of something quite delicious were wafting…

She stopped. "FangFang, they'll be really cross with me," she whispered, uncertain whether to saunter in or not.

Tell them you just went to pick up the chonkas, FangFang replied.

"Idiot!" she giggled.

At that moment she was spotted, and two dudey aunts came charging over, screaming her name and crying and smothering her with hugs. She almost wished they'd been cross with her instead.

Soon after, Jampa and the muleteers came into camp, looking completely exhausted. They'd been out searching all night.

"Sorry," she said sheepishly. She couldn't look at Jampa. He gave her a tired smile and said, "My happiness is your happiness." And nobody seemed anything but relieved that she'd returned safe and well. They'd even found her rucksack with the peace penguins thankfully still attached. While the aunts fussed around bathing her cuts and bruises and the cook served up huge amounts of pancakes with Nepalese bread and jam, she told them her story – leaving out the bit about the secret missile site that seemed to be causing all the problems.

After the stunned silence that followed she was forbidden to be out of sight of the aunts at all times. And Jampa organised a rota for someone to be on watch. "We can retrace our steps and head back to the village and inform the police," he said.

But both aunts insisted that to continue was the right thing to do. "The work we are doing is too important," said Aunt Yuhu. "And besides, I'm sure the local police wouldn't be able to do a thing – the politics of the Invaders is far too strong and powerful. We'll just have to be watchful."

"I've put an egg-of-light around Torma," said Aunt Ani. "That's more powerful than any pingpong politics."

Jampa wearily started packing up. "I'm afraid we can't afford to rest, so let's keep going. We've lost a day, so we'll now have to walk faster to get to the border to meet the minder. If we're not on time he won't be allowed to wait and it won't be possible to get into Tibet. The rules are strict. And tourists are often turned back and prevented from entering, even without being late."

Aunt Ani looked at Aunt Yuhu with concern. "We really *have* to get into Tibet. The future of our pingpong planet depends on it."

ANGELIC REALM

21

Abandoned

Jumpin' jellyfish! Where's that angel?

FangFang called and called, "Honey!" But there was no reply.

He carried on as if she was there anyway. "You're always on about manifesting whatever I want just by thinking of it. And how easy it is to order an angel. Then when I want to speak you're nowhere to be found.

"I want you to be pleased with me for helping with the magic mantra. And there's so much I need to ask you – like will I ever be able to get wings... And more about what I was before...

"Janglin' angels! I feel abandoned. If I could only know where I came from and what my story is, then I might feel better about things. It's all very well training to be an invisible guide. But sometimes I really miss having a body!"

Still there was no reply.

"Okay. I get it. Back to work in the Earth Realm..."

EARTH REALM

22

Run!

Torma found the fast pace tough that afternoon, as they hiked along the mountainside trail, high above the great river. She was relieved when they made camp on a narrow bit of flat ground – a stony patch beside a little stream on its journey steeply downwards. Everyone was exhausted. The mules were grumbling. Aunt Yuhu was calling her pink hat a crazy dimsim. And Aunt Ani was mumbling pingpong peace poems. Jampa had repeatedly tried to help Torma by taking her rucksack but she'd stubbornly refused to give it up, even after being stung by a bee. She was now feeling quite dizzy and faint.

Aunt Ani gave her a reassuring hug as they laid out the sleeping bags over the mattresses in their tent, saying, "Well done. We've put some distance now between us and the Geezer-in-Black."

Torma looked doubtful. She was sure that the Geezer-in-Black would be following close behind. He was just too…too nasty. He was an Invader.

"And anyway," Aunt Ani continued, "when you suffer on a journey it's a way of purifying yourself. And that's a way of purifying the world."

At this point, Torma didn't mean to, but…she vomited all over the sleeping bags.

Strangely there was no reply when she asked, "D'you think I'm purified yet, Aunt Ani?"

A little later they lay down to sleep, Torma with her head on the peace penguins, under less smelly but decidedly damp bedding, and listened to the sounds of the night. The gentle flapping of the tent, Aunt Yuhu snoring, the mules snorting, the river rumbling, and the veiled silence of the stars twinkling. Then, there it was, an eerie screeching howl – Mr Jackal calling to his family.

"Aunt Ani…" whispered Torma, "there's

something I've been wanting to ask you. Do you know anything about my father?"

"Torma-la, I'm sorry but I'm not allowed to say what I know. I've been sworn to secrecy."

In the dark a wandering tear escaped down her cheek. Years of longing to know mingled with the fear that seeped through her now. She was sure her father would be a great warrior and protect her from the Invaders. But his presence was as elusive as the sound of those stars.

She felt FangFang hug her heart.

If it makes you feel any better, I've no idea who any of my family are.

"We're best friends, FangFang. That's almost as good as family."

For two days they hiked up and down, climbing steadily, moving as fast as they dared with a numb, driven focus. They stopped only to place the magic crystals, chant and grab food and drink. All the energy was needed to put one step in front of the other. At one point the trail came down close to the great river, roaring and tumbling its force through open shingle banks before heading for unimaginably steep gorges. Torma watched the spray being thrown into the air as icy water challenged rock. It gave her some energy, but she shivered: "I'm pleased to miss connecting with the river this time."

On the third day they crossed over a large stream via a metal bridge where a cluster of houses gathered. The local men and women shouted "Namaste!" in greeting but didn't stop their work gathering dried grass and buckwheat, and storing various bits of wood and animal poo on their roofs. A woman spinning sheep's wool smiled at Torma through her door. Little children rushed up, excited to see the tourists, then became all shy. They were munching raw turnips. Torma felt she'd stepped back in time as she helped Aunt Yuhu give them pens and little notepads. It made her feel different from them. She would've preferred to run and play, rather than always having to behave like an adult. But a stern look from Aunt Ani told her to keep close.

Just stick your tongue out at her, said FangFang.

"Idiot!" she giggled.

No, really, it's a mark of respect in this part of the world, he insisted.

"No way... Why d'you think that?"

Sometimes things just seem familiar here. No idea why...

It wasn't until they'd crossed cautiously over the great river on a narrow, swaying rope bridge, climbed up and up across steep open pasture and through a stunted forest, that they came across anyone else. Smiling boys in maroon robes came running down to greet them. They'd arrived at a Tibetan monastery, even though not yet in Tibet itself. It was painted prettily with red and yellow patterns over long, white compound walls holding a central temple and long, balconied dormitories, with a beautiful white stupa outside. Torma clapped her hands in delight at being with others her age in such an obviously happy place.

She tried sticking her tongue out at the boys for fun and was excited to find they responded the same.

See! Friends forever, said FangFang.

The boys invited her to kick a ball with them and she introduced them to Speak Peace and Think Peace, whom they poked intriguingly. "Don't think anyone here has ever seen a penguin before," she told FangFang. "It's as rare as a yeti in London…"

It means the lost penguin will stick out like a sore flipper…

"It's a sore thumb, FangFang," she giggled

Penguins don't have thumbs.

"Idiot!…"

Then the boys showed her their stupa and they practised prostrations together. She was amazed at how slickly they carried them out on the rough ground, even without chonkas. It was on her third way around – her third kora as they called it –

that she suddenly felt uncomfortable. She knew she was being watched. Like FangFang she was sure of it, but didn't know why she knew it. She didn't see anybody else but the back of her neck felt prickly. It had to be an Invader. All the joy disappeared. The fear came back.

She felt like an animal… Hunted!

She didn't say anything to the aunts. They fussed quite enough already.

Moving on from the monastery, they walked up beyond the tree line onto wild open land scattered only with juniper bushes, and camped that evening near a cluster of tents gathered for summer trading. Locals were deep in conversation. Business was going on, swapping vital produce like salt, rice and potatoes. Torma kept away from everybody. She preferred instead the company of the mules. She sat on the patch of grass where they were tethered, and chatted to one with tattered brown ears and long eyelashes. He wasn't the leader with the bell around his neck, but he was the only light-coloured one, almost white – the one she felt drawn to.

"At least you know your mum was a horse and your dad a donkey. That's more than I know about my family," she said, feeding him some dried grass that had been blowing about, and stroking a soft ear. "But you need a name. I think I'm going to call you Fuel the mule. You do enough smelly poos along the way to keep an entire village in fuel for the winter."

Jewel might be nicer, came in FangFang, thinking that if this mule ended up as an invisible animal guide like the small deer then he'd need a wise name. There were times when his own name FangFang didn't seem quite important enough.

"That's a yuk name…too nambypamby for a mule!" Torma said, not forgetting being teased about her own name. So, Fuel it was.

"Fuel," she asked, "d'you ever wish you were free and able to roam in the wild?" Fuel eyed her knowingly. Torma took that to be a "yes".

"His work is his service to humans," said Jampa, who came and joined them, eyes smiling. "Anyway, I think he'd be eaten by the yeti." He pointed with his hand east to the grey rocks of the mountains, rising up to distant white peaks. "Over there…that land goes on forever. It's too high and desolate for people. Most of the year it's snowbound. That's where all the wild animals live – yeti, hyena, snow leopard, tiger…and of course, your jackal."

Torma looked searchingly across at the boulders that stretched off higher and higher into the distance. It was completely natural, untouched wilderness. The land of the yeti. It excited her. "I'd rather be chased by a yeti than an Invader," she muttered.

"Try not to let it get to you," said Jampa sympathetically. "That's what all the Tibetans have to do in their own country ever since the Invaders moved in. They have no choice physically. They're prisoners in their own land, and life is very cruel to them, but in their minds it's quite a different story. They can choose to live either in appalling fear or in compassionate joy. Most of them choose the latter. This shows great inner strength."

Torma thought about this over the yummy supper of eggs and rice insisted on by Aunt Yuhu, though she still missed ice cream. Then she managed to whisk some of it away to give Fuel some extra rations. It was gobbled gratefully, not without slobber.

They all lay at last in the tent. The sound of Mr Jackal's screeching howl was now somehow comforting to Torma. She was dead-tired after the day's efforts, but managed to ask sleepily, "Aunt Ani, you never seem to be scared. D'you choose not to be?"

"Yes, Torma-la. I surround myself with an egg-of-light and ask the pingpong angels to help. You can do that too, you know." But Torma had already been taken by sleep.

She awoke with a dream dancing in her mind. She was with Fuel and FangFang. She couldn't actually see them but, as often happens in dreams, she felt their presence beside her. They were exploring the wilderness, rising effortlessly up into the mountainous regions on friendly air-currents – dream-flying. The steep, rugged slopes and rough terrain meant nothing; the land was theirs to roam. She could tell that Fuel and FangFang were happy. They were all filled with compassionate joy. They were free.

Looking down, they saw a tiger playing with a hyena, and floated down beside them. A snow-leopard sat a little distance away, watching. The next minute something changed and a shaggy yeti marched in, standing up like a huge bear, snarling ferociously and threatening large, black claws. The other animals weren't scared. They seemed to welcome him. Torma wasn't scared, just fascinated. Even Fuel beside her wasn't scared. But FangFang was quaking with fear. "FangFang, it's okay. It's okay." She was shouting at him now: "It's okay!"

Aunt Ani was shaking her. "Torma-la, it's time to wake up. We've a long way to go today. We need to get to the border by sundown."

Torma shared her breakfast of Tibetan bread and peanut butter with Fuel as he was being loaded up for the day's work. She thought he carried far too much, but he seemed resigned to it. He looked at Torma fondly as he set off. She was sure he'd enjoyed the dream too.

Mornings were always cold, but this one dawned

colder than usual. The mountains were shrouded in heavy mist, enveloping everything in an air of mystery. What would this day bring? It was their last day in Nepal. That is if they were allowed over the border into Tibet. Torma jumped on the ice of the muddy puddles at the camp, cracking them into stardust. The day was beautiful but Torma was worried about FangFang. "Are you all right?" she called in her mind. "Why were you so scared last night?"

It took a while for him to come through, but when he did he said:

I think it's the yeti. I think I'm really scared of the yeti.

"But why?"

I don't know, but I intend to find out.

FangFang stayed with Torma for the journey that day, encouraging her to keep going. It was the hardest they'd had. It took them to the highest they'd been, right up to a pass at over four and a half thousand metres above sea-level. This meant that oxygen was limited and everyone was puffing and panting at the exertion. On and on. The climb was relentless. There were no trees now. In fact little vegetation at all. Just a few scrubby bushes from time to time. Mountain desert with bare gravel and dust eroded into deep valleys. So they were battling the harsh wind as well. This sapped any energy they had left.

There were times when Torma thought she couldn't go on. But FangFang would say:

Remember your mission to find the lost penguin and the heart of Tibet. You can't let Tenzin down.

And she'd feel a burst of effort as though a cool wind was pushing her physically up the mountain.

The dudey aunts would remind her to drink water and breathe deeply as they pushed their struggling bodies. And she'd watch them chanting and reciting the magic mantra, stopping only briefly to place crystals, encouraging themselves by saying, "We have to hold our silver river of light all the way to the high point on the great magic mountain. We have to speak the peace messages we bring. The Earth needs help. We will be there. We will not fail."

Jampa carried Aunt Yuhu's rucksack on his back and Aunt Ani's on his front. But Torma still wouldn't relinquish hers. Somehow it felt right to carry the important things that mattered, like the two little penguins and the chonkas...and the jam pancakes that the cook had made for them to take.

But it didn't change the fact that her feet hurt horribly and continuously begged her to stop, even though her thrashed and dust-ridden boots kept at bay the worst of the battering from the uneven stones. And her heels were well-covered with plasters, lessening the pain of blisters. But she'd no more have told the others that she was too tired to go on than eat a bowl of slug poo. She imagined herself at the highest point. She was not going to give up! Anyway, Fuel had done it, somewhere up ahead with a heavy load, so surely she must too.

It took them eight gruelling hours of climbing to reach the pass. Torma collapsed in a heap of relief at the flagpole there. It was held up by a pile of rocks and strewn with white silk scarves, blowing in the fierce wind along with faded prayer flags. There was no other colour anywhere apart from the cobalt blue of the sky. Just the greys and sand of the mountain desert in all directions. But wonderfully, straight ahead to the north, she saw a view to die for.

Let's get this mission done first, shall we? said FangFang. A body has its uses!

Torma was even too tired to tell FangFang he was an idiot. But ahead of them, across the deep valley of the great river now out of sight, mountains rose to the sky, topped by snow, like spoonfuls of ice cream. They were looking at Tibet!

"We should be in time for our rendezvous with the minder tomorrow morning," said Jampa, smiling. "But we've got to keep going to get down to camp at the border-post this side." Wearily Torma picked herself up, struggled through a couple of prostrations, just to please the aunts, and trudged on.

Prostrations only work if you have the right intention, said FangFang. *I can see the dullness of your vibe-catcher.*

"Shut up, FangFang!"

He watched her vibe-catcher brightening dramatically as they headed downwards. She now had the energy to look around. There was only gravel and stone and rock in varying shades of brown and grey. It was barren raw Earth. No, Torma decided, it was more like they were on the moon. But there was something about its naturalness which she loved. She felt completely part of it. It was wild and free. She joined the aunts reciting the magic mantra and understood somewhere inside herself that the nature fairies were there too. It made her feel beautiful. All around was beautiful…a bit like the compassionate joy she'd felt in the dream.

Before long she could see down to the great river, now pale turquoise, carving its way through this dramatic landscape as it had done for aeons. It led her gaze down to a gathering of bright blue blobs, the painted tin roofs of the houses at the border-post. Civilisation. Or so it seemed after days on the trail. But it still took three and a half weary hours to come steeply down the thousand metres in height to reach it.

The tents were pitched in the hard dirt, held down with rocks against the fierce wind. They were outside one of the blue blobs perched on stone walls grandly called a hotel. At one end a draughty shack had a tap in it. The dudey aunts became wildly excited at the idea of a shower, even with icy water, but then inexplicably changed their minds. It could've been something to do with the shower bucket, which had a dead rat in it.

Torma would have had a shower but had other things on her mind. She discovered that the muleteers and the mules were not going to cross the border with them, but would head back tomorrow, the way they'd come, along with the cook. This was upsetting news. She didn't want Fuel to leave. The aunts had given the men some money to thank them. She could hear them already spending it on chang, the local beer, in the hotel. But what about the mules? How could she thank them?

After wolfing down a welcome supper of Tibetan dumplings known as momos, with hot chocolate, the aunts couldn't wait to climb into their sleeping bags. Torma struggled to keep awake until she was quite sure they were asleep and then, grabbing her jacket and hat, crept out of the tent. She almost turned back when she felt the bitter cold. The night sky was sharp and clear with a thousand stars and the glow of a moon behind a lone cloud. It made her less afraid. But it was FangFang's C'mon, we can do this which gave her the courage. How good it was to have her best friend with her.

Careful not to be seen, she slunk from shadow to shadow, away from the tents and down alongside the buildings of the street. A dog barked. She froze. But then all quietened. She was sure the mules would be down here somewhere. But where were they? Then she heard a familiar snort and the tinkle of the bell of the lead mule. She saw their shapes tethered tightly against a falling-down wall. She spotted the light colour of Fuel. He looked miserable. "Don't worry, Fuel," she whispered, softly fondling his ears. "Remember the dream. You'll soon be wild and free." She picked up the tether rope and with difficulty managed to get her cold hands to work on the knot. At last it released. He nuzzled her. She pushed him away. "Go, Fuel. Go, before you're discovered!" Suddenly she realised that the other mules were on the same rope.

Why not let them all go?

She hadn't meant to...but okay, what the heck?

Torma knew she should return quickly in case she was missed. She melted quietly back into the shadows. But worryingly, she could see better now – things like the shiny bits of a motorbike at the side of the street and the great river shimmering. The moon had appeared, bright and full, with a silver halo around it that reflected on the mountains beyond as though there were vibes around them. Tibet! The way forward tomorrow. Just for a moment she felt a connection with them. Just for a very short moment.

Suddenly there was a shout in her mind:

RUN!!!!

Before she could react, a familiar, vice-like grip had grabbed her from behind, pinning her arms. A hand reeking of garlic over her mouth. "Gotcha! You leettle rat!!" hissed the Geezer-in-Black. Torma tried to stamp on his foot. But he was wised-up to it this time. "Oh no you don't! You're going to deesappear. No one weell ever know what happened to you. Zere's a lot of suffering waiting wiz your name on eet!" Torma madly tried to kick and scream and punch. All to no avail. He gripped her tightly in his huge arms. Then turned her over and dragged her down the street, growling. "We're going to start off weez a good wheepping." His voice was drowned out by an approaching noise. "Here come my men…"

She was helpless.

ANGELIC REALM

23

How Did I Die?

Watching a large person dragging a small one had an effect on FangFang. It reminded him of something which was drawing him away. He knew he should be helping but kept on wondering what it actually was that was drawing him away. Janglin' angels! Could this have been how he'd died before he became an invisible guide?

He couldn't do the job he was meant to be doing while he was thinking about himself. And anyway he should make the most of Honey not being around, just in case she'd stop him from doing what he had to do. He'd been obsessing about what had happened to him before. He needed to find out now.

"Nope. No sign of Honey. Coolish. Now what had she said about visiting the great library where the 'book of life' is stored? 'Like everything you just imagine it strongly and you will be there.'"

FangFang tried to do everything right.

"Okay. Here goes… Firstly I need to be calm. Jumpin' jellyfish! that's not going to work. Part of me is on duty in the Earth Realm, which is not exactly calm at the moment. Never mind. I'll try the egg."

He practised picturing the egg-of-light around him. Before long he was surrounded by a lovely, rounded, egg-shaped bubble of light.

"Uh-oh! Got it! Now. I imagine the great library which holds the 'book of life'. I imagine it as a huge white building with tall pillars and glass sides and sunlight pouring in on shelves and shelves of books."

And suddenly there it was. Easy as pie. Just as he had imagined it.

He walked in through the immense see-through doors, which seemed to be made more of cloud than anything else, and along wide, open corridors filled with shining beings with wings neatly folded, all studying the books. His gaze was drawn to what appeared to be the centre of the building, where an enormous book sat on a golden plinth. Hovering above it was a sign… 'The book of life'. An angel in glasses, which appeared to be more for show than anything else, walked down the steps to meet him. "Welcome, FangFang. What would you like to know?"

FangFang decided he wouldn't get involved just now in how the angel knew his name, so went ahead and asked, "Please…I'd like to know how I died."

In a trice he was whisked into a situation as though in a dream. He was in a dry riverbed. Standing up like a huge bear, almost as round as it was tall, a hairy beast with long black claws was snatching him and dragging him along. There was screaming. Then he was flying through the air and landing in a hollow of rough stones. Thump! The next minute a giant foot with long black claws came down heavily on him. Plonk! He was aware of fear. Then nothing. Not even pain.

FangFang could see the beast looked ferocious, but could also see what was in its mind. There was no malice at all. Only interest. And dismay that FangFang had been trodden on. Uh-oh!… He'd been squashed accidentally, it appeared.

But what was the beast? There was no doubting it… It was a yeti.

He'd been killed by a yeti!

At this point the connection seemed to go. The great library faded. FangFang had a fleeting sense of Honey Angel brushing past him and then vanishing again. His awareness was back in the Earth Realm.

EARTH REALM

24

Nothing is as it Seems

The Geezer-in-Black, dragging Torma down the street, was wrong. It wasn't his men approaching.

Down the street at a thunderous gallop came a herd of mules, the dust behind them picked up by the moonlight like a cloud of dragon smoke. Snorting and puffing, heads pushing up and down, ears flapping, bell clanging, braying loudly, they came. At their head was a light-coloured beast, teeth bared. (If you've ever seen an angry mule like this you'll know to keep well out of his way!) He crossed the dusty gravel in a flash. Pushed past where the Geezer-in-Black was dragging Torma, and lashed out to the side with his hooves, again and again, as only mules can. There was a crunch. The Geezer let out a yelp of pain and fell. Torma found a hand and bit hard. Then wriggled out of the tight arm-lock and, quick as a flash, rolled to the side, as the rest of the herd pushed past, trampling legs and arms in their stampede.

Torma ran.

In two minutes she was back in the tent, climbing breathlessly into her sleeping bag. Aunt Yuhu turned over and murmured, "You should've done a wee before…"

In the morning the muleteers left to return to the high village after dropping all the kit off at the border gate. Apparently the mules had broken their tether in the night and rampaged around the border-post ransacking food supplies and causing outrage: "Mules can't be trusted!" and "The muleteers should have been watching them!" But they'd all been rounded up. All that is except for one – the light-coloured one. No one seemed to have seen him.

Jampa was to accompany the dudey aunts and Torma over the border and on around the magic mountain, for which they would hire yaks to carry the kit. That at least comforted Torma a little at the loss of the mules. But first they were to be met by the minder with a mini-van to go through the border controls.

The border sounded formidable. Jampa told the aunts, "If we're going to get through we have to be careful. The Invaders will search us thoroughly. If they find anything that they think might threaten their security, like books or pictures they don't like, then we'll be turned back. The last two tourist groups didn't make it." The aunts deleted photos on their cameras and abandoned a couple of books. Torma was sure she had nothing threatening in any way. Penguins weren't threatening, were they?

The time came. They were all nervous. Both the missions – the opening up of the portal of light for the Earth and the quest to find the heart of a country and the lost penguin – depended on getting through. Jampa led them across the great river on a narrow, swaying bridge and then through a metal gate. This was it. They were in. Torma couldn't understand what all the fuss was about. She sat down while waiting for the minder with the van to pick them up. She looked at the great river, now the same, but she was looking through a tall fence with barbed-wire rolls along the top. That was when she was hit by an overwhelming sense of sadness. A minute ago she'd been free.

Now she was in an occupied country controlled by armed soldiers. She was well aware that all the Tibetans, including her great grandparents and Tenzin, had suffered immeasurably. Her heart felt broken. Tears rolled down her cheeks unchecked.

You're picking up all the pain of the Tibetans, said FangFang. Even the nature fairies cry here.

From the moment she set eyes on Liupee, the minder, she was scared. He was a typical Invader – well-fed tummy, black hair, sallow skin, dark glasses and a domineering way about him. He never smiled. "Passports!" he ordered in Invader English, and then, "Get een ze van". They were all taken, along with their kit, a few hundred metres up a tarmac road to a huge, ugly concrete building, which looked all wrong in this wild mountain desert. Here, ten Invader officials with guns insisted they open their bags and tip everything out. They then spent the next couple of hours going through it all and asking silly questions – about all the photos on the cameras, the medicines, the smelly clothes…

Torma wished she could pour sackfuls of slugs down their trousers.

They took things away to investigate; the maps; the cameras; the yeti book; even a tennis ball which Aunt Yuhu used to massage her back; and, worryingly, the purple bag of printed peace messages. Aunt Ani became really concerned. Torma tried not to look at her. She knew she was carrying the rest of the precious crystals hidden in an inner pocket of her fleece. Torma felt a big lump of dread in the pit of her stomach.

Suddenly an order was barked. "Zeengs back een bags." Then they were shoved back into the van along with Jampa.

"Why's everyone so rude?" Torma asked Aunt Ani.

"Shh," replied Aunt Ani, a finger on her lips. "It's 'cos they don't like anything Tibetan."

"But why?" whispered Torma.

She could only just hear Aunt Ani's reply. "'Cos they're afraid of the Tibetan magic."

They were driven a few miles up onto the Tibetan Plateau, a vast area of sparse grassland which stretched for hundreds of miles in all directions. "Keep an eye out for a lost penguin who lived with the nomads," Torma whispered quietly to the peace penguins. It was indeed the home of the nomad – at least until the Invaders started removing them... Huge billboards covered with Invader writing lined the side of the road. There was no one else around. No other tourists. No other vehicles. Even the friendly great river disappeared into an eroded valley. An empty feeling.

Then the road unexpectedly became fringed

with green willow trees and they entered a town. Torma stared in amazement at the sudden change to rows of concrete houses and shops hanging out gaudy plastic items, and dozens of Invaders and their families driving along on what looked like lawn-mowers, going about their daily lives.

They were taken through big locked gates into a compound with broken glass on the walls and asked more customs questions and sat waiting for hours for what appeared to be paperwork. Torma was bored and restless. It didn't look like they were going to be able to leave this town. While no one was watching, she wandered down a corridor aimlessly. Glancing through an open office door, she saw a woman talking heatedly with a man. The woman pushed the door shut. But not before Torma had seen that the man had his arm in a sling and was using crutches to stand up. Torma couldn't be sure, but there was a whiff of garlic…

Returning to her seat she saw Aunt Yuhu handing Liupee wads of money.

"What about the peace messages?" asked Aunt Ani. "He said we'll get them back…"

"Let's just get out of here now," replied Aunt Yuhu.

Thankfully, soon after, they were allowed to go. Liupee ordered them into the van and drove them north out of town. They were on the way!

Torma saw it first. "Look! There it is!" They'd been driving across featureless plains, wide open spaces to the horizon in all directions, with herds of yaks and Tibetan chiru, the wild antelope, grazing on brown grass, when suddenly a shining white pyramid appeared to the north, like a mystical stupa. It was the unmistakable top of their magic mountain.

"Stop! Please stop," pleaded Aunt Ani. "We have to honour the spot of our first pingpong sighting."

Liupee kept on driving as though he hadn't heard.

"Stop, you crazy dimsim!" yelled Aunt Yuhu. "I really have to take a photograph."

Liupee still kept on driving as though he hadn't heard.

"Stop! Please stop," muttered Torma quietly. "I need to get chocolate out of my bag in the back. You can have some if you like." The vehicle screeched to a halt.

It cost her entire supply of chocolate, but she had a couple of happy aunts who were able to surreptitiously place a crystal and chant the magic mantra while Torma managed prostrations, taking care to hold the right intention of the words.

They had connected with the mountain.

Now they could see that close by was a great lake. It stretched far into the distance, grey and wild, whipped by the wind into foaming wavelets, and watched over by large numbers of water birds. The sun came out from behind scudding clouds and picked up shining slices of water. Torma stared in amazement as she watched the sheen of the lake turn to a deep, turquoise blue. Puzzled, she turned to Aunt Ani, who had her finger to her lips. Raising her eyebrows, Torma mouthed the word "Magic?" and saw that she had guessed right. So the work they were doing was able to change the energy of this special land.

Jumpin' jellyfish! FangFang shouted. Janglin' angels! You wouldn't believe the light coming off the lake!

Torma knew something was unusual. She had a sense of goldenness at the edge of her vision.

"It bodes well for the mountain," said Aunt Ani, smiling.

"Een ze van," barked Liupee, bored now that the chocolate had been devoured.

As they drove further north towards the mountain there was more traffic and many more of the huge billboards. They came to a wider tarmac road and then, suddenly, squared streets, surrounded by buildings, hotels of sorts, and trading stalls. This was the kora town from where all the pilgrims set off to hike the circular route around the magic mountain, eventually arriving back in the same place. It had a commercial, rough feeling about it. There were men hanging about drinking and playing betting games. And dark-green-clad soldiers swinging guns aimlessly. Torma didn't feel safe at all.

They were driven into a small compound, and Torma and the aunts were shown one of the dimly lit rooms around the edge with a smaller room off it, which would have been dark if not for a small, high window. It was grubby and smelt damp. What passed as toilets were smelly holes in the centre of the compound, behind low concrete walls.

"This is not what we booked!" Aunt Yuhu said indignantly. "We've paid for a hotel room with a shower."

"Wait here," growled Liupee. They sat on wonky plastic chairs beside a dirty old table and looked at each other. What was going on?

Liupee returned with a woman dressed in the dark blue uniform of the Invader police. Torma gasped. She was sure it was the woman she'd seen in the customs building speaking with the man on crutches with his arm in a sling.

"You can have zese back," she said in Invader English, dumping the purple bag of peace messages onto the table. Thwack! Aunt Ani smiled thank you. The woman glared at her as though she didn't exist. "But zere eez change of plan. Zere's no longer permeession to hike ze mountain trail. You wait here unteel Comrade Liupee can arrange transport to drive you across to ze ceety of Lhasa, where you weell fly out of ze country. Your Nepalese guide weell stay to feed you while you are here, and zen he weell be sent back to hees country ze way he came. You weell not be allowed out of zees compound, for your own safety. Have a nice day."

She nodded to Liupee and marched out of the room. At the compound gate she stopped and spoke with two burly policemen settled there, guns at the ready.

There was no doubting it. They were under house arrest. They were not going anywhere in a hurry. Aunt Yuhu was muttering angrily, "Crazy dimsims!" Aunt Ani just sat with tears pouring down her cheeks. They knew the impossibility of their situation. Also the precariousness. If they made a fuss, Torma, being the one with Tibetan ancestry, might quite possibly not be allowed out of the country and the chances were high of her never being seen again.

Torma didn't move. She sat, stunned, aware of how important it was to the aunts and what their work meant for the planet.

A dejected Jampa brought in some blankets and some rice and eggs for dinner. Even this couldn't lift them. They ate in silence, each in their own misery. Each too tired to think straight.

Torma moved into the back room to collapse on the grubby bed and read her book. The only one she had left after the border confiscations. Her eyes were sleepy. She could feel FangFang being busy in her mind. But she was too tired to take much notice and dozed off.

Waking with a start, she sat up. Had FangFang woken her? She searched in her mind.

There was an idea lurking…

ANGELIC REALM

25

In Trouble

Honey Angel was waiting for FangFang. He knew he was in trouble.

"There's always a good reason for not knowing things," she said, not unkindly. "When you chase your own story you're not able to do your guiding job properly."

"Sorry," said FangFang. He didn't like to say

"Well wouldn't you want to know if you'd been stamped on by a yeti?" She just seemed too...too shiny to worry about things like that.

"The chief angels are concerned," Honey Angel continued. "Our girl is on a very important mission and they're not sure you're able to support her in the way that she needs. We can find an easier assignment..."

"Uh-oh!..." The thought of being taken away from her was too much to bear. "Please, I can do it... Please give me another chance."

"All right then."

"Coolish!"

"So... As we know she's not good at calling the angels for help, remember to keep her safe by putting an egg-of-light around her. Make sure you pause beforehand to let the love intention come in. It's like striking a match in the Earth Realm – don't rush it. Bringing light is the most wonderful tool."

FangFang felt himself so surrounded by light that it melted him into a blissful state of compassionate joy. He was determined to get it right this time.

EARTH REALM

26
Alone

Torma tried to catch the idea that was floating around in her mind.

"It's my fault we're in this situation," she thought to FangFang. "If I hadn't let myself be caught by the Geezer-in-Black, the dudey aunts would be allowed to hike the kora." She felt shaky. Scary butterflies were bumping around in her tummy.

"So… So…I have to do something about it."

I'm right with you, said FangFang. Maybe it was the way he said it but she immediately felt calmer and less scared.

"So, how am I going to get out? I've been thinking about that window…" By the soft light of the moon, she could make out the high window, almost brown with filth but with a broken catch. It was very narrow, but quite long. No adult could get through, but she was no adult. It would be a tight fit. Involve wriggling. But how to get up to it? "I think I can stand on the bed-end and work my way through… Right. Decision made."

She was about to try when FangFang stopped her.

You need the things that give off light.

"What? Ah, of course. Oh help! This is not going to be easy."

She crept into the other room where the aunts were sleeping. Thank goodness Aunt Yuhu was snoring loudly. Grabbing the peace messages on the table was no problem. But the magic crystals were different. They were in Aunt Ani's fleece in her rucksack on the floor, right beside her head. The slightest sound and she would wake up. Her crystals were the thing most precious to her. She would be attuned to them.

"FangFang, I can't do this." Torma whispered.

I've got it! I'll distract her in a dream.

"However are you going to do that?"

I don't know. But it sounds a great idea.

"FangFang, be serious."

Have you got a better idea?

"All right then. Go on."

Aunt Ani seemed to smile in her sleep. Torma grabbed the rucksack as quietly as she could. Took it into the other room. Collected the bag of crystals from the fleece pocket. Then replaced the sack beside the bed. Back in her own room she breathed out. So far so good. Now for the really tricky bit.

Stretching up from the bed-end on tiptoe, she grabbed the ledge of the window, pushing it open. First she pushed out the messages and the crystals, then her boots and even her jacket, thinking how proud Granny would be that she had remembered her jacket. But the thud, thud, thud, thud was terrifying. She was sure her heart was beating even louder. Would someone hear? Oh, hang on…

Quickly she climbed down and grabbed the blanket, forcing it into her sleeping bag on the bed to make it look like there was a body there. Then back to the window.

Pulling up on the ledge, she launched herself up off the bed-end with all the strength she could muster, scrabbling with her bare feet managing to find some friction on the rough wall, until she was pushing down on the ledge with her hands and her arms were straight. This raised her body to the height of the window, bringing her feet up so she was crouching on the window ledge. She'd seen that move, known as a mantle-shelf, on a rock-climbing film once and had tried it out later on the kitchen cupboards when Granny wasn't looking…

The next bit wasn't as easy as she thought it would be. She grabbed the sides of the window and with a lot of wriggling, got one leg and then the other through, till she was sitting on the ledge. A bit more wriggling of her body through… Then luckily there was just room to twist around at her narrow waist, so her hands could hold the ledge to lower herself down as far as possible. The window clinked shut. Then one more thud.

Phew!

She held her breath. And listened. She could hear dogs barking somewhere. Otherwise, all seemed quiet. She'd made it! Gymnastic skills certainly had their uses. She pulled her boots and jacket on, taking care to turn the bright-pink colour onto the inside.

"Oh poo! I've forgotten my rucksack, and that means the peace penguins too." Well, she could stuff the crystals into the jacket pocket, but she had to hold on to the purple message bag.

Looking round, she could just make out that she was on the edge of town in a sort of wasteland.

That was a good thing. But she couldn't resist creeping along and peering round to the front of the compound. There was a fire burning low and the burly policemen were lying beside it, fast asleep.

Coolish! came in FangFang. But stop messing around and get out of here.

"Which way do I go?"

Away from the dawn.

She knew that was right. The dudey aunts had often spoken about the importance of hiking the kora in the traditional manner – that is, walking around it clockwise, which most people did. So, as the town was in the middle of the southern end of the magic mountain kora, then the start meant heading due west. In the other direction were faint pink rays of the sunrise. Already small birds were calling. Soon the town would be stirring.

When would her escape be noticed? She imagined that Jampa would bring early cups of tea. But maybe they'd let her sleep in a bit, which would give her some time.

Maybe they'll realise what's happened and cover for you, said FangFang confidently.

"More likely they'll panic and a herd of crazy dimsims will be summoned... Anyway, let's go. I need to get warm."

It was bitterly cold. Torma's boots crunched on the frosty ground even though she tried to go quietly. Also, she couldn't help blowing on her numb hands. Spotting two figures plodding slowly along what looked like a trail leading out of town she walked over and joined the rough path, keeping a good distance behind, thinking it would look less suspicious if she went at a steady, pilgrim rate. She would be one of many.

But she was alone on the kora.

The sun was up and casting long shadows before she reached somewhere that sheltered her from the eyes of the town, a large pile of sacred stones, known as mani stones, each beautifully painted with Tibetan mantras. She gratefully squatted to place one of the crystals and chant the magic mantra. And then started the prostrations, which proved painful on her hands without the chonkas – something else she'd forgotten to bring. But she knew she had to do prostrations with each placement, and was determined to do it all in the manner that the aunts would want.

"I hope I'm doing this right, FangFang," she said. "I know it's important."

It's the intention behind that counts, he said. I can see from your vibe-catcher that it's okay. The silver river leads onwards...

The way ahead was marked by a huge moon, in spite of the daylight, tinged red and hanging low in a crystal-clear sky. "That's an auspicious sign if ever I saw one," a Tibetan voice behind her said suddenly. It startled Torma so much that she jumped up, looking around her in panic. A man dressed in a Tibetan sheepskin tunic, known as a chupa, was looking at her. He led a shaggy yak, decorated with red wool on long horns, carrying bundles. A woman in a long chupa and Tibetan apron then arrived.

"Tashi delek, hello. Did Pala give you a fright? Sorry. Come and join us. I'm Amala. We're about to have breakfast." Torma slipped happily into communicating in the Tibetan language as if she was talking with Granny.

Pala laid out a string of prayer flags on the stones. They fluttered brightly. "We like to show respect to the nature fairies," he said. "Those of sky, clouds, fire, water and earth – shown by the colours of the flags. It's important to fly them. Then peace and harmony for all beings are spread on the wings of the wind. We can see the wings with our hearts…"

They sat on a rock and unpacked a flask of butter-tea, pouring some into a bowl of porridgy-looking stuff – roasted barley known as tsampa. Rolling it around in her hands till it was mixed, Amala offered some to Torma, asking her name.

"Thu je chey, thank you. I'm Torma," she said, politely bringing her hands together on her heart, and ate, not knowing what else to do. Then she drank the butter tea offered. Normally she'd have gagged at the yak butter and salt in it. Today it seemed the right thing to drink.

They didn't ask questions, but just sat comfortably. Pala spotted Torma's bloodied hands and rummaging in the bundles produced a pair of old worn chonkas. "Here, take these. Looks like you need them."

The Tibetans were so naturally loving it made Torma want to cry. Not now, she told herself. Don't cry now. At least she could give them some sort of a reason as to why she was on her own. "I'm looking for a penguin," she said, as if that would explain everything. A soft-toy penguin." Then she giggled, which made them laugh too. It felt good to giggle.

"Actually," said Amala, "we did hear tell of a penguin…"

That was the moment Pala saw soldiers approaching. "Looks like we've got Invader company."

Torma grabbed the chonkas and the purple message bag and fled.

She ran uphill away from the trail to a large rock and from here ran on behind more rocks till the incline of the hill meant she couldn't be seen. Still, she ran. There was so little cover that she had to put some distance between her and the soldiers. Panting hard, she pushed on, though her legs were burning, and still onwards.

Eventually she collapsed and lay on the spiky grass, chest heaving. Hopefully no one was following. She couldn't see… But suddenly there was a piercing scream behind her that set her heart beating even faster.

Spinning round, she was confronted by a sand-coloured animal who looked like a cross between a giant hamster and a furry slug, so fat that he could barely stand on his hind legs. "Hello," she said. "Are you a marmot? Sorry to disturb."

The marmot turned and dived into a nearby burrow. Quite enough disturbance for one day.

She was sorry he disappeared. It would have been nice to have chatted more. This was his home. And somehow he reminded her of Tenzin's words 'my country is my land, my family…part of me…' and she had a feeling Mr Marmot could have shed light on finding the heart she searched for…

Gathering her breath, she sat up. "Oh my goodness, there's a view to die for!"

I've told you about this before, said FangFang.

"Idiot!" came the reply.

She could see the kora trail far below, leading up a vast half-pipe valley carved out of sand-coloured rock, with fans of loose stones – the scree fields. There was no doubt the nature fairies were in charge here. Nothing covered the rawness of the Earth. Towering high above it all was the shining white pyramid of snow. The mesmerising magic mountain.

She knew it was forbidden in Tibetan tradition to climb to the summit, but still she could almost see steps up it, as though it was calling her. She felt something inside her reaching out. There was a connecting of hearts. An acceptance. An understanding of harmony at her being here. It made her happy. But still she knew it was important to honour the mountain. So she did prostrations using the new chonkas, and placed a magic crystal.

For the moment she could see how to stay high, following the trail below by moving towards a large, flat ledge. She was looking down to where pilgrims were going through a brightly painted archway that looked like a stupa, towards a tall flagpole. Hopefully, if she moved carefully, she wouldn't be seen from below. Surely all eyes would be on the mountain itself. There was very little vegetation now. Mostly she scrambled over rocks, and managed to traverse a steep incline, arriving gratefully at the flat ledge.

But the sense of relief didn't last long. She was hit by a strange, eerie feeling.

FangFang was upset and saying Jumpin' jellyfish! Again and again.

Jumpin' jellyfish!

There was an uncanny hissing noise, and looking

up she saw numerous sand-coloured vultures with long neck-ruffs and large, pointed beaks circling overhead. Tripping over something, she looked to the ground. That was the worst of it. She was staring at scattered bones...

Human bones!

27

Letting Go

"FangFang, it's okay," said Honey Angel, wrapping him in comforting angel wings.

"Janglin' angels! Seeing the bones makes me miss my body. I think I have a problem with letting go of it."

"When beings come over to the Angelic Realm the bodies they leave behind aren't important any more. It's like moving house or changing clothes. All physical things are impermanent. They come and they go."

FangFang wasn't convinced.

"What matters," continued Honey Angel, "is the kindness and lovingness that is brought. You're doing well there."

"Uh-oh! I'm getting involved in my own story again, aren't I, Honey?" said FangFang.

"You'll get it. Don't worry."

FangFang sighed. But he really enjoyed the hug.

EARTH REALM

28

The Cave

Torma knew about Tibetan burial grounds, of course. Granny had spoken of them, and of how the Tibetan Plateau freezes too hard for digging graves and is too high up for trees, so there is no timber for fires to cremate bodies. The natural way to dispose of bodies is to break them up and ask the vultures to come and feed. It's a way of being in harmony with the nature fairies. And Granny had explained that it's all done respectfully, burning incense and chanting mantras, after the being has flown from the body to the Angelic Realm. And anyway it's being generous and compassionate to the vultures. But it was still a shock to be here.

She hastily chanted the magic mantra as respectfully as she could and backed slowly off the ledge. She felt sure it was a forbidden place. Hope I haven't offended anyone, she thought. Most of all, hope I haven't been seen.

"FangFang, are you okay?" she called in her mind.

All this body stuff makes me wish I still had my body...

"Oh FangFang. Just think, if you still had your body we couldn't be best friends and we wouldn't be doing this exciting adventure together. And I couldn't do it without you. I'd be far too scared."

That makes me feel so much better...and all filled up with love for you.

"And I'm all filled up with love for you. I've never said that to anyone before."

Now you're getting really soppy...

"Idiot!"

Torma hadn't noticed while they were talking, but now she suddenly spotted dark-green figures climbing up the hillside towards them. Invader soldiers!

"Oh poo! C'mon FangFang. Let's go. All this being hunted is getting boring."

Which way to go? She definitely didn't want to go across the burial ground. Maybe she could go back the way she'd come and give up this whole crazy journey... Doubts were creeping in... Maybe... Or perhaps she could find a way straight into the mountain, which was mostly sheer cliffs. She might be trapped, but there was also a chance there could be somewhere to hide.

No time to wonder, so she headed towards a narrow cleft in the cliff, which looked as if others sometimes passed that way. It led to a steep field of loose scree, which she scrambled up with no worry of falling – only of the stones which tumbled noisily towards her pursuers.

After a while the gradient eased and it bent to the left, so she was hidden from view. But looking around at the terrifying cliffs unfolding in all directions with no apparent way through, she despaired. "FangFang, there's nowhere. I can't see anything to do."

I'm putting an egg-of-light around you.

"How can that possibly help?"

Just at that moment a crow flew in, cawing loudly. He hopped onto a large boulder and disappeared behind it. She peered over and saw him strutting about in front of what appeared to be a marmot hole, or was it a shadow? No, definitely a very narrow hole, though no one could tell.

Just what she had been hoping to find.

"Thank you, Mr Crow," she said, as she scrambled up onto the boulder and slipped awkwardly down the other side, squirming herself into the hole. Pushing her purple bag and chonkas in front of her, she wriggled along a cold dark tunnel. It smelt damp but she could definitely feel air moving through it, which was encouraging.

Eventually it turned a corner. Here, she stopped and tried stilling her breath. She'd always wanted to know what it felt like to be a slug, or even a hamster. Now she knew what it was like to be a marmot.

There was a deep silence. If there was any talking at the entrance she couldn't hear it. And she was pretty sure that no normal adult would be able to follow her inside. Even so, she didn't dare move until her legs started getting stiff and cold.

"Hey, FangFang, we're right inside the mountain," she whispered. "How exciting is that!"

Coolish! And the egg-of-light worked, he said.

"Can't see how."

It was the nature fairies who responded to the love and called Crow in.

"Okay. Thanks anyway. He certainly looked like he knew his way in…" She suddenly stopped…

She could almost see her hand. It was very

dim, but there was some sort of light. It had to be coming from inside the mountain! She crawled further along. The light became brighter. And brighter, until the tunnel opened out into a spacious cave and she could see that the light belonged to a yak-butter lamp.

She blinked, not so much at the brightness as at the surprise before her eyes. To one side the flame of the lamp burned on a rock altar alongside items of dull metal. On the other there were collections of dusty papers neatly stacked. And then in the middle, a low box with a faded carpet on top. Sitting cross-legged and very upright on this was a skinny old Tibetan monk with long, grey hair and a face that looked as crinkled as the mountains outside, wearing nothing more than tattered maroon robes. He didn't move but spoke quietly in a croaky voice that sounded as though it hadn't been used for some time, "Tashi delek, hello. I've been expecting you."

She was too stunned to say anything.

Then questions came pouring out.

"Tashi delek. D'you live here?"

"I am here."

"What d'you eat and drink?"

"I live on life-force."

"What d'you do?"

"Meditate."

"How d'you keep warm?"

"Inner fire."

"How long've you been expecting me?"

"Since the beginning of time."

She gave up questions. They didn't really help. Tibetan magic had really got her stumped this time.

Then he asked her, "Did old Crow lead you in? Feeds on compassion that one. Likes to be of service to the yetis."

Torma nodded, wondering if Mr Crow thought she was a yeti.

"Come… Sit with me."

There wasn't anything to sit on, so she arranged the message bag and chonkas on the dirt in front of him and sat down, emulating him – straight-backed and cross-legged.

"Concentrate on the lamp."

She remembered looking at the lamp. At the flame flickering and bending. The different colour at the edges. Then spiralling. The next thing she was dream-flying. FangFang was by her side along with a sense of shining beings. They were floating above the magic mountain, looking down at its perfect shape – a snow pyramid with dazzling rays of firelight stretching out to rock buttresses and then radiating out beyond… Further…further… carrying light to the far points of the planet.

A silver river waited nearby.

Being here was easy. All sense of time had

ceased to exist.

She had no idea if it was seconds or days, but suddenly she was back in the cave. The old monk hadn't moved. "See...the old compassionate heart of Tibet has not been lost... The world has need of it...when ready."

How did he know she was looking for the heart of Tibet? She wasn't sure...but had a more pressing question: "Was I really flying?" Though she instantly regretted asking that one.

"Are you really existing?" was the enigmatic reply.

She had no idea of the answer. But she did know that her doubts about whether to carry on with the crystals, the peace messages and the prostrations were completely gone.

"It is good that you continue your quest. I have been waiting for this. When the portal of light has been opened, I shall go."

"Go? Go where?"

"To the Angelic Realm. My body will dematerialise."

"You mean you won't need the vultures?" Torma stared at him in awe." Your body will just disappear?"

There was no reply. His eyes had shut. His breathing had become very faint. In the soft light of the flame, burning low, she could see a look of complete peacefulness spread across his old, worn face. It was time to leave.

"Thu je chey, thank you," she whispered

Squirming back out of the tunnel and over the boulder Torma stood stock-still. It was dark. How had she spent that long in the cave? In one way it was useful for not being spotted, and hopefully she would be able to creep past the soldiers and get a good way ahead on the kora, but the way down to the main trail was steep and slippery on loose scree…

"FangFang!" she called in her mind. "FangFang! Where are you?"

There was no reply.

Now she felt very alone.

Heading out and down the steep slope she kept stopping and listening to the night. There were a thousand stars overhead, clear and cold, which gave some shadowy light. She could pick out the lighter-coloured rocks in the valley, and even the small river which meandered near the trail, though no moon yet. Okay, she could make out the direction to go. More or less straight down. What was that scratching sound? Was it the wind? Had the soldiers been waiting here? Was she being watched from below? She couldn't see any camp lights anywhere.

Her foot loosened a stone, which clattered speedily down the slope. Heart in mouth she stopped again. All was quiet. She was scared and cold, hungry, thirsty and tired, but dared not linger.

The next bit was the steepest... Careful, careful, where to put her feet? Then a flush of wings and something huge flew close... Shady Forces?... Vulture?...

In a panic she rushed...and fell.

Head-over-heels... Rolling...falling...

ANGELIC REALM

29

Lost

FangFang didn't know where he was. Except definitely lost. "Uh-oh!… Jumpin' jellyfish!"

He'd gone joyfully on the dream journey. The view from above the magic mountain had been spectacular. He'd never forget how it looked… Magnificent…dramatic…glowing – an ethereal beacon sending light out into the world as though with its own huge vibe-catcher.

Then, when the call came to return to the cave, somehow he'd thought he'd just see briefly what else there was beyond…and kept going… following the light over the mountains, across the plains, further and further towards the ocean. There he'd found a family of dolphins dancing and playing in tumbling surf and couldn't resist the fun. For a while he'd stayed with them, then, wondering what was over the horizon, had flown onwards and onwards until huge ice fields had appeared and he'd hung out with waddling penguins for a while, content and happy.

Then guilt had overtaken him. He'd been thinking only of himself again. Now he wasn't sure how to get back. He knew he should be able simply to imagine himself where he needed to be, but the worry about being lost seemed to have taken over.

He was reluctant to call Honey. He'd be in trouble again.

EARTH REALM

30

The Precious Present

Falling, tumbling like a rag doll, Torma slid the complete length of the scree field, banging her shoulders, knees and, worst of all, her head. She landed. Squelch! in something softer and smellier than rock. Then she blacked out.

She came-to with a pain in her head as bad as she'd ever experienced, and groaned loudly.

"Shush, shush," said a voice. She was dimly aware she was being carried over someone's shoulder, and then thankfully blacked out again.

When she next came-to she was in a dark-brown tent. Her head was throbbing badly, one shoulder was agonising and a knee felt as though it didn't belong to her body. There was smoke around, which smelled of yak-poo fire.

As her eyes became accustomed to what was outside the pain of her body, she realised that someone was holding a bowl to her mouth. She tasted Tibetan butter-tea. And there was a wet cloth being held to her head, smelling of tangy herbs and stinging like crazy. "Ow, that hurts," she complained.

"Hey, Torma-la." A kindly face smiled at her. It was Amala. "Don't try to talk. You're okay now. Pala found you – in a pile of marmot poo as it turned out, which saved a nasty landing! And he carried you down. He'd been watching out for you. We knew you were on the mountain somewhere."

The realisation dawned. She was safe. Tears came to her eyes. She couldn't help it. Amala gave her a hug, which hurt her shoulder, but she didn't care. She was safe. Just for the moment she didn't have to be in control and grown-up.

"Ah, little Torma-la," said Pala lovingly, which made her cry more. "We had to watch for you. We knew you'd be in trouble the minute you told us your name. Torma means 'precious present'. Most people bring a precious present to the mountain. You brought yourself. There's no bigger gift. But giving yourself comes with pain."

"Oh." She tried to sit up. "But I brought peace messages... I need to find them..."

"It's okay. They're here. You were clutching them. And the chonkas."

"But the soldiers..."

"We will look out..."

Once again it seemed Amala and Pala understood what was going on without having to be told.

She relaxed and shut her eyes.

"Sleep now, little Torma-la."

She awoke to the sound of the wind flapping its wings through prayer flags. There was packing going on. "We must move... Soldiers," Amala said, quietly helping Torma dress in a thick Tibetan chupa and sash, exactly her size, with room for the peace messages and crystals in the front pouch. And some drop-dead-gorgeous red-felt boots. Then she braided her hair Tibetan-style, fixing in beautiful turquoise and coral stones. And wrapped a wool scarf around her face.

"There. You look properly Tibetan now."

Torma noticed that Amala gazed at her with tears in her eyes.

She explained. "These clothes belonged to our

only child, our daughter. She died last year. The authorities wouldn't let us take her to hospital. She died..." Amala swallowed back tears. "Now, we're hiking the kora for her."

Pala put his arm round Amala. "And now they will help Torma-la. They are a gift of life."

"For the new daughter the mountain has given us."

Torma had never felt such a lovely sense of being a family – a deep sense of belonging. They helped her place a crystal and chant and manage a few stiff prostrations. Her head throbbed painfully, but her heart sang.

They rolled up the yak wool tent and placed it with all their bundles on the yak. Then they lifted Torma up on top. She didn't think the day could get any better. Her thoughts even took her far away to how good it'd be to tell the kids at school about riding on a yak. Funny how sometimes the most pain can bring the most joy.

"Thank you, Jack the Yak," she whispered, sinking her face into the long hair at his high neck and stroking the brown fur underneath. He smelt of earthy, burned chocolate, of long-suffering and of toughness. A rough grunt came back, in between snatching mouthfuls of the mossy cushion plant that grew in clumps in this near-desert land. She curled up on his back and Amala put a heavy rug over her as Jack trundled off, swaying from side to side.

If soldiers passed them she didn't know, for she slept, even when Amala and Pala stopped to place the magic crystals and do prostrations. Her body was healing Tibetan-style. It was as though the mountain nature fairies were looking after her, rocking her gently in their arms. Up high, the west face of the magic mountain smiled down on them. Eyes of rock, steadfast and powerful, watching through the ice…holding her.

All day they travelled, Pala leading Jack the Yak, Amala walking behind, following the trail along the west valley of the kora. The only others they saw were Tibetan pilgrims, some doing prostrations, some just ambling. Foraging chiru antelope with big horns passed by, little sparrows visited. The way was barren and open, inviting the wind to blow fiercely, picking up dust to rasp bare skin as though claiming this wild land for itself.

By afternoon the trail turned away from the sun and they started climbing, still following the river. Torma awoke feeling better as they crossed it higher up, with Jack splashing his way through and Amala and Pala jumping from rock to rock. A little further on she was surprised when they came up to a building – a monastery. It was deep chocolate-coloured, with gold trimmings on top. Behind were multiple layers of prayer flags. Lined-up in front were little white stupas.

Mr Crow was there to greet them, looking official in his black suit. He dive-bombed Jack repeatedly until Pala said, "Okay, we'll stop. Let's set the tent on the far side of the monastery."

I wonder if this is the spot, thought Torma. She turned to the magic mountain. The dome of the north face shone with a fierce light in the clearest blue sky. Its presence filled her with an awe that made her very bones feel naked. It had to be the spot.

"This is the powerful place where the heart of the mountain is exposed to the world." said Pala. Here, since time began, any wish that is said for the good of all is bound to be granted."

So this *was* the spot where the dudey aunts had planned to speak out the peace messages. It had to be done.

After they'd made camp they walked slowly up the long steps to the monastery, mindful of sacredness. It had been built around a cave where hand and footprints of high monks were embedded into the rock. Torma accepted magic without question now. Rules were different here.

They sat in the lamp-lit cave and offered the nature fairies the light from the peace messages and a magic crystal. The air was thick with benevolent power. The abbot and his monks then brought them butter-tea and invited them to climb onto the roof. Here they joined them doing prostrations honouring the mountain light from the north face. Then they chanted as a bright full moon appeared, adding to the strange glow in the sky. The peace messages were spoken out, many in a Tibetan accent, and the wind came and took them on its wings.

If FangFang had been watching he would've seen the light spoken from loving hearts, multiplying a thousand-fold…spreading out to the far points of the planet.

"You have made us very happy, little Torma-la," said Pala afterwards, as they sat round the fire in the tent eating tsampa and yak cheese and drinking more butter-tea. "We have been of service to all beings. Our lives have meaning."

Then Amala cuddled Torma, who told them her story, and they listened with acceptance. She had the feeling that whatever she told them, they would love her just the same.

"And will you hunt for the penguin?" Amala asked.

Torma giggled happily.

"It was the nomads we spoke to at the trading post on the road to Lhasa," Amala continued. "They were the ones who'd heard tell of the penguin. If you go past, ask the old man at the café there. He'll be able to tell you. It was his grandson Bodhi who knew.

"Okay. I will." Torma didn't really want to think

of the future just at the moment. The present was too precious. She quietly whispered, "Thank you Amala. Thank you Pala. You're precious to me." Hearts overflowed in the darkness.

Outside, the mountain continued to glow. The night was bitterly cold. But they snuggled to sleep, warm in their Tibetan clothes and thick rugs as the fire burned low. The air was full of love. Torma felt completely and utterly at home.

They were at five thousand metres above sea-level where the air is thin, so they expected breathing to be hard. Amala coughed a lot in the night. But towards dawn Torma woke, sensing something had changed. She could still hear the wind flapping its wings through the prayer flags, but it was Jack coughing this time. She pulled on her boots and crept outside.

There were just the faint stirrings of daybreak from across the mountain. The stars were still clear as crystal. It was so cold she could see her breath freezing. She went and cuddled Jack who was lying outside the tent, cosy in his thick coat.

"What is it, fella?" He nuzzled her and she stroked his nose as he blew warm air onto her. Then she saw.

There were lights coming up the trail on the far side of the river. Maybe six or seven of them. They were heading this way. Surely pilgrims wouldn't be out at this time. Were they soldiers? FangFang would know. Where was he when she needed him? They had to be soldiers.

If she was recognised, she knew that Amala and Pala would be in serious trouble.

She knew what she had to do…

And it broke her heart.

Pala had said being the precious present would be painful.

31

Everything Works With Love

"Honey Angel! Honey Angel! I need help."
FangFang had finally got the better of his pride.
He was fed up with feeling lonely.

Immediately, she was right there with him.

"Uh-oh! Honey. It's as though you were there

all the time."

She smiled her sweet, honeyed smile. "It's okay to ask for help. Remember?"

"Janglin' angels! I'm sorry but I think I got distracted. Then I couldn't work out how to get back."

"Did you forget to do it with love?

"Jumpin' jellyfish! And the egg-of-light…"

"Oh, FangFang. Never forget: everything works with love. C'mon. Our girl's about to have a tough time. She still never thinks to ask the angels for help. She needs you."

EARTH REALM

32

Storm up High

Crouching outside the tent, it wasn't Pala's words, it was Tenzin's from oh so long ago that haunted Torma. "Being hunted freezes the heart."

She knew about pain. In one way or another she'd been used to it since her mum died when she was a baby, and never having known her dad. But here in Tibet life had shown her how to open her heart and love deeply. And now she had to find a way to stop feeling, which was something she didn't want to do.

"Thank you, Jack," she whispered longingly. Tears fell and froze on her cheeks as she checked she still had the important things she needed in the pouch of her chupa, then slipped quietly behind the tent down to a stream. She felt sure it would lead around out of sight and join the main trail further up after the north face. Trouble was, it meant having to cross the main river, now covered with a layer of ice. Would it take her weight?

She jumped from boulder to boulder where she could, but then she had to tread on the ice itself. All went well until the last step to the bank. There was an ominous crack and her left foot smashed through into the water... Oh poo! She was more concerned about wrecking her lovely red boots than the consequences of wet feet in this bitter cold.

A familiar voice came in to her mind.

Going for a swim, are we?

"FangFang! Where've you been?"

I've been travelling. What's been going on?

"I nearly died!"

Coolish! Keep trying. You'll make it one day! It's fun here...

"Huh! And I found and lost a family."

You've got me. I'm your family.

"Yay!… And we sent out the peace messages."

Uh-oh!… So I didn't miss much!

"FangFang! I missed you. You idiot!" He exasperated her, but at least it made the lump in her throat go away.

She hoped the climb would bring some warmth. She was as cold as she'd ever been, particularly her left foot. Once she'd joined the main trail the way led continuously upwards. Normally this wouldn't have mattered, but her head was banging so badly that she struggled, whether from the fall or the altitude she wasn't sure. But she had to take a frustratingly slow, steady pace, glancing behind to check she wasn't being followed. Thankfully, no sign of soldiers.

Unusually, a white cloud hung in the sky above the gleaming mountain. What did that signify? She was attuned to Amala and Pala's way of taking meaning from the natural world around her – the messages from the nature fairies.

Every so often she stopped to place the magic crystals, counting out how many would be needed before reaching the high pass, which she knew was the sacred place where the final crystals had to be placed. And she chanted as she placed each one and did the prostrations. This actually warmed her somewhat and her left foot didn't feel cold any more.

But the wind continued to rise and a couple of

exhausting hours later she sank down to shelter behind a boulder, painful head in her hands. She realised then that the reason her foot didn't feel cold any more was because she couldn't actually feel it at all. It was numb. Oh poo! She didn't know much about frostbite – just enough to know that people's toes went black and then dropped off. Oh poo! Poo! She was so miserable she didn't even have the energy to cry.

You've got to keep moving!

"I can't give any more."

I'm imagining you there… FangFang felt as though he knew the way. He could see it. C'mon! Imagine it!!

"I can't find how to…"

C'mon! You can do it.

"I just want to curl up and go to sleep."

Do it for the dudey aunts. Do it for Amala and Pala.

"I'll try…for them…"

She found a piece of yak cheese in her chupa pouch, which gave her some energy. Then reluctantly dragged herself up and kept plodding on upwards. It seemed to go on forever… Higher and higher…step up, step up…drag one foot… then the other… Every step upwards made it harder to breathe. Surely the high pass would be here soon.

At least it was easy to follow the trail, which

twisted and turned through mani stones. But she realised that the colour of everything had changed to grey, and it was now harder to see anything, as cloud had come in. Also, it was snowing. Not nice, fluffy snow, but hard, sleety stuff that stung her face. That must have been the warning of the little cloud this morning. She pulled her scarf tighter round her head.

Her mind was going numb too. Too numb to imagine where she needed to be... Wandering and unsure...on and on...up and up...dragging step after step... Now white underfoot – maybe she wasn't really here – maybe falling down a steep slope in the dark... Or being chased by soldiers, relentlessly on and on...walking on one leg as the other one had gone...

I'm here with you, insisted FangFang. It's okay. Earth needs you to do this. It's important.

Taking time to hold the love, he held her in an egg-of-light.

Her mind let in more positive thoughts... On and on, up and up, dragging step after step through the snow... And rather a warm tent beside a fire... drinking hot butter-tea...cuddling a furry friend... Prayer flags blowing in the wind...

Prayer flags? She could hear prayer flags! Then she could see wildly bright colours, refusing to be dulled by the grey cloud. They were everywhere, streams and streams of prayer flags sending messages out on the wings of the wind, flapping and beating ferociously. This must be the high pass! The highest point on the kora! The sacred power point!

"FangFang, look, we're here!" Tears of relief stung her eyes. She searched around through the sea of flags to find what felt like the right spot. A spot that wouldn't be disturbed. Moving away from the trail towards the forbidden central zone of the mountain she found a sheltered hollow, filled deep with snow.

Using a rock, she cleared the snow and laid out the magic crystals that had been specially programmed for this, the final point of the river of light, high on the magic mountain. Then she covered the crystals with rocks, more and more, until a little stupa stood where the hollow had been. Then she chanted and chanted till her voice was hoarse. And wearily did prostrations in the snow alongside, ignoring the cold which penetrated her body, concentrating only on holding the energy of love, honouring the light.

It was done.

As she finished, there were flashes of lightning. And thunder rolled round and round as though the mountain was celebrating. It began to snow heavily. She could barely see anything now. The blizzard was taking over.

Do the magic mantra, said FangFang.

She had no energy left to question or even be afraid. It had taken everything she had. She lay in the snow gasping for breath in the thin air, numb with cold, with no idea which direction she should go in or what she should do. She may as well recite the mantra. The nature fairies would help.

"Caw! Caw!"

There, strutting about on the stupa, was Mr Crow. He flew off, wings carving through the storm, and then stopped, looking back.

You must follow, urged FangFang. Trust!

It took a while for the messages to get from brain to body. Here, at nearly six thousand metres, there was only half the amount of oxygen she normally breathed. This was doing funny things in her head. Her brain felt it was on fire and trying to get out. But eventually she managed to roll over and crawl after Mr Crow.

He took to walking so she could follow his delicate footprints, just visible. Then, as the gradient became easier, she managed to stand up and stumble along, tripping over rocks, fighting the wind which threatened to blow her to the ends of the Earth… Trust…. Trust… Head drumming, feet and hands numb, throat dry… Trust… Heart beating fast to catch the oxygen… Trust… Trust…

She had no idea how long it took, but they came to a narrow ledge which looked like it headed off a cliff. "I can't go along that!" Trust… Trust… She went onto hands and knees again and crawled, not daring to look to the edge, where wild currents of snow whipped the nothingness of fury beyond... Trust... Trust.

Then Mr Crow disappeared. She moved towards where he'd been. There was a dark opening. Moving in, she stood up. Her eyes adjusted to the gloom. It was a large cave. Quite sheltered from the storm. The floor was well packed down with footprints. Large footprints with scratches that could only belong to long claws. Some looked fresh. One end was scattered with porridgy poo. The other had flattened piles of dried grass. There was a strong, wild, pungent smell.

Jumpin' jellyfish! said FangFang. This is a Yeti cave...

ANGELIC REALM

33

Celebration

"There's something I want to show you," said
Honey Angel. "Come, see."

FangFang found himself enfolded by Honey
Angel's wings and flying at the same time. They
flew up and up through the buffeting and swirling
storm, until completely free and dancing with
the stars. On all sides there were soft flushes of

golden wings. They were flying in a host of angels!

He was sure he'd never felt so blissful, so totally part of all that is.

"Look down," Honey Angel told him.

He could see Earth. Green and brown and large swathes of blue, with swirls of cloud painting flowing patterns. Immediately he was drawn to one mountain range, where a vibrant light blazed out, so bright everything else appeared dark.

He wondered if angels ever had to wear sunglasses. Then immediately regretted it as he remembered that angels could hear all his thoughts. There was chuckling.

He felt Honey beside him. "The portal is open. There's great celebration," she said. "And you helped. Well done."

He didn't feel pride this time. Just compassionate joy.

"And now," she said, "much-needed light is able to come into Earth via the portal."

He felt happy for Earth. For all beings.

"But you must return. There's learning to be had in the yeti cave. There's always joyful work to do… And we have to welcome a great being who's joining us."

Honey sent FangFang a picture of the first cave where the old monk had sat. All that remained now on the faded carpet were fingernails.

EARTH REALM

34

Where is Safe?

"Thank you, Mr Crow," Torma said, now safe from the storm in the cave. "From now on I'll trust that all is well." Even so, her eyes searched the dark corners carefully. It seemed no one was at home. It was empty. She was also safe from the yetis – hopefully sheltering somewhere else tonight. But, she knew there was one essential thing to do for survival.

Gathering rocks into a circle, she pulled out the purple peace message bag from the pouch in her chupa. Yay! The aunts had included a tiny peace candle with a box of matches. Scrumpling the papers inscribed with all the messages she placed them in the rocks, added dried grass and then dry porridgy poo. She struck a match and held it to the messages. It blew out. The next match blew out too.

Pause and hold it lovingly, said FangFang.

She tried again, with a pause, and saw light. And held her breath. The flame bit. Smoke wafted. She watched as slowly a fire took shape, then added more poo. She had heat.

Now she understood that sometimes to have poo is to be rich.

The purple bag seemed waterproof, so she used it to gather some snow from the mouth of the cave and placed it beside the fire. Before long she had a system of water to drink and gulped greedily. Never had water tasted so good. Soon her headache eased and she could think about what to do with her left foot.

Peeling off her boot she placed it on the rocks, now warm. Her foot looked waxy white, not black. Well, that was good. But it still had no feeling in it. She rubbed it with her hands, again and again. Still no feeling, though her hands felt better.

Finally she decided to put the foot awkwardly in the purple bag of warm water. Still nothing. Then, after a while, she started feeling tingling, and then pain. Such pain as she'd never ever experienced. She shouted in agony, which made her feel better. Slowly, slowly the feeling came back in her foot. Phew!

Warm at last, though feeling week and woozy from hunger and lack of oxygen, she piled up the fire with poo and snuggled into the dried grass. The blizzard howled loudly outside, tempered only by the gentleness of falling snow.

"FangFang, you're on yeti watch," she murmured. And slept.

FangFang was deep in thought. His journey to the stars had changed him. He understood then that yetis were indeed part of all life. That all beings had their place. Sometimes they helped others without realising it, sometimes they didn't. They just existed. It was love that made the difference.

Torma awoke to complete silence. The wind slept. Rays of pure sun reflected off new snow and poured into the cave. Today was a new world. But hunger drove her to move. She drank all she could, said "Thank you, yetis" and headed out.

The narrow ledge she'd crawled in on last night was now covered in extremely slippery ice. It sloped worryingly away towards the cliff edge. Well, she thought, as long as there's something for my hands to hold I can keep my balance. She was halfway along when she realised there wasn't… and she couldn't. Suddenly she was falling. She just had time to say "FangFang, you'll be pleased…" when she landed, Whhham! in a deep snowdrift. "Oh. That didn't hurt. I think I'm still alive. Fun!"

FangFang giggled. All was well with the world this morning.

But Torma wasn't too sure how to get out. She stood up, shoulder deep in a vast snow bowl. Looking back up she could see that further on from the ledge she had fallen off were icy rocks, so she had actually taken the best way down. This trust thing was quite good. But now it was time to wade. Luckily, her long boots were perfect, and the new snow was soft, but it was hard work. She pushed slowly onwards to a lip of the bowl, where she was able to climb out and get a perfect view of where to go next. Far below she could see down beyond the snow to what had to be the east valley, the last section of the kora. She could join the trail there. First there was a lot of snow-sliding – "Yay!" – then steep scrambling downwards.

Within a couple of hours she had left the snow behind and found the trail. There was no one else in sight. Or so she thought.

Suddenly, out of nowhere, Invader soldiers were surrounding her. She couldn't understand what they were saying but felt sure it was "Gotcha!

We've been watching you come down. We've orders to bring you to the kora town. You will come with us."

"Oh poo!" But she knew sometime or other she had to allow herself to be caught. And now the crystals had all been placed it didn't matter any more. And anyway, they might help her back to the dudey aunts. And, importantly, they might have some food.

She was surprised to see that they were all young men, not much older than herself. They were obviously trained not to show any emotion, but didn't seem to be naturally nasty or aggressive. Good.

"Have you got anything to eat?" she asked, indicating her mouth with her hand.

They shook their heads. She sat down on the stony track to show that she couldn't move. She saw the soldiers look at each other. One of them had softer eyes than the others and produced a flask, pouring hot water into a packet of noodles and offered it to her. She smiled at him. Perhaps this being captured thing wasn't going to be so bad after all.

After the third pot of noodles she was ready to go. And started walking with them. Now in the eastern valley it looked fairly flat all the way to the town – not too strenuous.

Except FangFang had other ideas.

I think you shouldn't forget this is still a pilgrimage. You should be honouring the Tibetan way and holding light for Earth by doing prostrations. I'll hold you in an egg-of-light.

So she stopped and pulled the chonkas out of her chupa pouch. "I bring peace with my actions, my words and my mind." She slid down flat out onto the rough track. "I lay down the suffering of the planet." Head touching the Earth, hands up, say the Tibetan mantra, stand up. Take three paces. Do the magic mantra. Start again.

There was a gentle flush of wings and Mr Crow did a farewell fly-past. Way up high a mountain eagle soared over them, as though king of the winds. He seemed to be watching over the beings in his territory…

The soldiers looked at each other in amazement. This didn't look like the criminal girl they were expected to pick up, but a proper pilgrim. They were too stunned to do anything about it and walked along at the slow prostration pace.

When the soldier with soft eyes gave Torma some water to drink she tried speaking to him in Tibetan. "Well, why don't you join me? You're not going to be beaten by a girl are you? You're so nambypamby." This was too much for him. He obviously understood Tibetan. He pulled his gloves out and did prostrations too. Torma turned to the others. "You know it'll bring you merit and purify all your bad deeds."

By the time they reached a rock band of beautiful green and pink stone, every one of the seven soldiers was doing prostrations. Torma wondered what bad deeds they were worried about.

Hour after hour they worked together, sliding down, standing up, three paces forward, hundreds of times, moving slowly, focusing on the intent of benefitting the planet, even the soldiers it seemed – melding into the zone, like a team on a sports pitch concentrating on the moment where all physical discomfort disappears, giving way to the greater good.

Tibetan pilgrims passed them. They stared in disbelief. No one had ever seen an Invader soldier do prostrations before.

It was midnight before they reached the town. But not too late to process criminals.

Torma was taken to the Invader woman police chief who stared at the soldiers covered in dirt from head to foot. Torma was sure she stifled a smile. But then the soldiers' officer came in, straightening his clothes. He was cross at being dragged out at this time of night, but knew the military should always take pride in immaculate appearance. He took one look at his soldiers and exploded in anger.

Any merit they might have gained from

capturing the criminal was lost. Torma tried to explain that it was her fault but was told to shut up with a harsh order that sounded like "Lock her up securely. We will deal with her in the morning."

And so Torma found herself taken back to the compound – the one which now had windows firmly boarded up. She hadn't minded facing the Invader policewoman. It was facing the dudey aunts that worried her. The burly policemen on the gate shoved her back into the room. The aunts woke up with a start. They looked drained and frazzled.

"Aunt Ani! Aunt Yuhu! I'm so sorry. I've caused a lot of problems for you…"

"Torma-la! Pingpong Torma-la! You're okay! We've been so worried about you," Aunt Ani shouted in delight. "My! How Tibetan you look!"

Yes, Torma felt Tibetan from the top of her beaded hair to the tips of her well-scuffed red boots.

Aunt Yuhu started fussing around. "You must drink water and you must eat this rice and I'll make you hot chocolate." Torma looked longingly at the window…

"We're doing our own cooking now." She continued. "The crazy dimsims sent Jampa home. He left you a message to say 'You are special among thousands.'"

He had the brightest vibe-catcher, said

FangFang.

She would miss Jampa and his kindness. He would've smiled at what she'd done.

She told the aunts, "I did it, you know. I placed all the crystals in the right way. And the peace messages have been sent off correctly. It was all my fault that you couldn't do it. I'm so sorry, I thought it was the only way…"

Aunt Ani took Torma's hands. There were tears in her eyes. "Dear child… Don't be sorry. You've been very brave. It was no doubt all as it was meant to be. I know you were doing the kora for us all. I had pingpong dreams about it every night."

Coolish! It worked, said FangFang.

"Idiot FangFang!" Torma giggled.

"And I know that you completed it successfully," Aunt Ani continued. "I was in meditation yesterday and saw that it had all been done in a state of pure love. The portal was open." She hugged Torma. "Now the Shady Forces will be overcome and the Earth will be safe."

"We're so proud of you," said Aunt Yuhu, and hugged her too.

The kora was complete.

"Now all we've got to do is get you safely home."

When a stink of garlic in the shape of the Geezer-in-Black hobbled in on his crutches the next morning, they realised that was not going to be so simple.

35

Too Many Rules

"Whatever did you do on the final kora section?" Honey Angel asked.

"Uh-oh!… I'm sorry I got over-enthusiastic and the egg-of-light became too big and covered all the soldiers as well," FangFang giggled.

"Well, that might not have been such a bad thing," said Honey, but the chief angels may have something to say about it. Your assignment is just with our girl. As her guardian angel I can allow you to work with her in any way, but that doesn't cover other humans around her. Which includes interrupting other humans' dreams, by the way. When you're more experienced things may be different. We have to keep things in natural harmony."

"Jumpin' jellyfish! Too many rules…"

"Rules help everyone live happily together…"

EARTH REALM

36

Penguin Search

In the compound the humans weren't exactly living happily together. There was an argument going on. They were speaking in Invader language and Aunt Yuhu, who understood most of it, being from Hong Kong, was translating quietly to Torma.

"I'll take her from here," barked the Geezer-in-Black. "She's a threat to national security. She knows too much." Being a bigwig in the Intelligence Bureau he expected people to jump to attention immediately, but somehow, having his arm in a sling and relying on crutches undermined his authority.

"She's my responsibility," The Invader woman police chief insisted, as Aunt Yuhu translated. This was her territory. She was not going to let some upstart plain-clothes geezer take over from her. She didn't like being posted to this dismal desolate place. If she made a success of it she would be returned to civilisation.

"No! She's my prisoner. Keep off!" The spotlessly clean military officer ordered. He had the reputation of being the supreme power around here. He couldn't lose that. And it was important to make amends after his men had come in looking so dishevelled last night. They were now of course locked up, and would be facing severe penalties.

Liupee appeared and, though he was a lowly tourist guide, thought he had better mention that his company had contracted to look after these tourists and it was crucial that their good name wasn't tarnished, so their country might not lose face overseas. The honour of their country was at stake.

It seemed there was an argument going on.

Aunt Yuhu was horrified, and began pacing up

and down wringing her pink hat in her hands. Aunt Ani sat looking sad. They both knew they were a hair's breadth away from Torma being locked up and never seen again.

However, Torma herself was highly amused.

"FangFang, the entire might of the Invader army and police has nothing better to do than look after me!"

You're so important, Miss Tibet, he giggled.

"Idiot!"

After much heated slanging the woman police chief won. Her uncle was a bigwig in the government. It was decided that the military officer would provide two soldiers to guard Torma and the aunts while Liupee drove them across the plateau to the city of Lhasa, where they could stay in a posh hotel and then be put on the plane out of the country.

Torma looked at the Geezer-in-Black, who was scowling. He was the one she was scared of. She had no doubt at all that this would not be the end of it.

The dudey aunts couldn't pack up their things quickly enough. Within the hour, Liupee had bundled Torma, the aunts and the two soldiers into the minivan and they were driving away. He was very pleased with himself. He'd managed to negotiate a good deal for his tourist company and would probably get a promotion out of it, and an increase in salary.

Torma looked longingly back at the magic mountain. She really missed the simplicity of being there with the nature fairies and Amala and Pala, where everyone looked after everyone else. It had made her feel so completely at home.

Tibetan heart beating?... suggested FangFang.

"Hmm..." said Torma, wondering... "It's certainly different from the way these Invaders live... Why are they so concerned with their own importance? It seems so...so not-real."

Well, the vibe-catchers of the Invaders are mostly dull and grey. Except for when the soldiers were doing prostrations for the planet and they became alive with light. And the woman police chief had some light in hers when she insisted you catch the plane. She was being compassionate.

"FangFang, sometimes you're so useful..."

I'm a super-duper under-cover agent...an uh-oh spy!

"And sometimes you're an idiot!"

Torma turned from FangFang in her mind to talk to Aunt Ani. "I feel bad that the special chonkas from the chief monk in Kathmandu didn't go round the kora. That was important to him."

"Don't worry," Aunt Ani said. "His gift was the meaningful thing to him. He would understand, as the intention was good. But all things change. That's pingpong life. Anyway, the chonkas have had an interesting journey, no doubt sending their own good vibes out."

"Can things give vibes out?"

"Yes, sometimes. If they've absorbed them from beings with good vibes."

"Cool!"

It gave Torma something to think about on the long and rough road. She wondered if she could put good vibes into the two little penguins, Speak Peace and Think Peace, who she was now happily reunited with... She cuddled them as the road went on and on. This was big country. Mile after mile of rough grassland, with only dust-whirls and families of yaks to see, following the west river valley. Then she settled into eating. The aunts shared the rice and momos they'd brought with them, while Liupee and the soldiers ate noodles. She needed to make up for the days of not eating on the mountain anyway.

After some time she saw they were coming to a marketplace where families of nomads had laid out rock crystals, yak cheese, fish bones and bowls on blankets in the dirt. This must be the nomad trading post. Ah! The café. How could she make Liupee stop here? All he'd said so far was, "No stops. We keep going!"

Sitting behind him as he drove she was able to

lean over the back of his neck and shout, "Please stop! I'm going to vomit!" He obligingly came to an abrupt halt. He must have changed his mind.

Before anyone could react she climbed over the aunts, threw open the door and rushed out of the vehicle, past a group of sleeping dogs and into the café. There was a woman wiping down a table.

"Bodhi's grandfather?" Torma asked hurriedly. She could see Liupee approaching through the window... The woman pointed to an old man sitting at a table playing dice, who smiled and waved her over.

"I'm looking for a penguin."

"A toy penguin?"

She nodded, holding her breath...

"Of course, it's only what my grandson overheard... There was talk of a penguin taken by a yeti. Went off dragging it behind him like a trophy, so he said. No one's seen or heard anything since..."

Torma was about to ask further when Liupee's hand grabbed her painfully by the arm, with a soldier on the other side, and they dragged her back outside. "Stay een ze vehicle eef you want to get out of zees country alive," grumbled Liupee. "You're more trouble zan you're worz."

That was the least of it.

It all happened very quickly.

There was a screeching of brakes, a dusty old

jeep drew up, engine revving. Out jumped four men. They punched Liupee in the face, hit the soldier with the back of a gun, grabbed Torma and shoved her into the jeep. The driver pulled out a gun and shot the tyres of the minivan. From the back of the jeep the Geezer-in-Black leaned out of the window and shouted, "Don't bozer to chase us. We're taking her to Lhasa preeson. No one comes out of zere."

There was a spinning of wheels on the rough gravel. The second soldier pulled his gun and shot through the hat of the Geezer-in-Black, narrowly missing his head, but sending the hat flying out of the window. The Geezer-in-Black ducked his now very bald head down close to Torma. She promptly vomited all over it. The driver put his foot down and shot off, swerving around a herd of yaks, tearing off in a rain of bullets and barking dogs.

"You leettle Tibetan rat!" yelled the Geezer-in-Black, wiping sick off his bald head with what he thought was a towel but turned out to be his jacket. "Why can't you come quietly like normal creemeenal?"

Torma shut her eyes tight, trying to pretend the last five minutes hadn't happened. That all those guns hadn't gone off. If she sat very still perhaps she'd be able to believe that she wasn't sitting next to the Geezer-in-Black. But she could smell his garlic breath even on top of the vomit.

"FangFang. Are you there?" she asked.

There was no reply. Why did he always disappear just when she needed him?

"FangFang!?"

Where was he? Then she remembered, at least she had some positive news about the penguin. "FangFang, did you hear that the penguin was dragged off by a yeti?"

There was still no reply.

Indeed he had heard…

37

Definitely Unusual

Surely there had to be only *one* being who had been dragged off by a yeti.

And FangFang had only *one* thought. To get to the 'book of life' in the great library as quickly as possible. Never mind rules. He had to know. He focused on the egg-of-light with difficulty. It was hard to hold the love strongly enough, but finally he managed to find himself at the great see-through doors. He marched in single-mindedly, with barely a glance at all the other angels and the rows of wonders. And up to the golden plinth. The angel with glasses greeted him warmly. "Welcome FangFang, what would you like to know?"

"I'd like to know who I was before I died," he said firmly.

In a trice he was whisked into the dream like a TV news-clip. He was being cuddled lovingly by a tiny girl in a nomad tent. She offered him some of her tsampa for breakfast. Then they went outside into the sunshine to play. The next moment there was pandemonium – soldiers, shouting, fighting, running – and he found himself hiding out with the tiny girl in a dry river bed.

He could see what he was…

He was a very grubby, faded, pink and purple, fluffy penguin!

The yeti snatched him out of her arms and dragged him…

FangFang couldn't watch any more. He felt as though he'd been hit by a sledge hammer. He was a penguin! He was a penguin! All his dreams of being some great warrior came crashing down. They meant nothing! All he was was a small penguin… not even a real one…

He was a soft-toy penguin!

He doesn't remember what happened next.

Just that Honey was beside him, wings hugging comfortingly.

"Uh-oh! Honey. It's so dreadful. I know… I can't be. It's not possible. I mean.. I don't want to be.. I can't be a penguin… and not even a real one… NOoooooo!"

"This is why it was important that you didn't know," she said. "It's a shock, but you will be able to accept it."

"Jumpin' jellyfish! Never…! "

"You know many of the great invisible guides are animals," she said. "They bring a beautiful energy of service."

"But not soft-toy animals…"

"Yes, that is definitely unusual."

"Janglin' angels!"

"You know FangFang. It doesn't matter what you are… It's the love in your heart that counts."

EARTH REALM

38

Behind Bars

"Well, you leettle Tibetan rat. Zees ees ze Lhasa preeson. You weell join ze ozer rats here." The Geezer-in-Black sneered triumphantly as they drew up at the large metal gates of a vast concrete compound. It had an air of coldness, impregnability and finality.

Torma had managed to draw into herself for

the long, tiring journey across the plateau and then into the city, where there were surveillance cameras on every corner.

"I'm already in prison. You Invaders have made the whole of our country a prison," she sneered back, knowing with her whole heart that this was indeed her country. She certainly wasn't going to give him the satisfaction of thinking she was afraid of him. Anyway he didn't look so scary without his hat. And with a bald head.

She was aware of countless stories of Tibetans who'd been sent to prison for no reason other than loving Tibet. Some had come out. Most had not, but on each and every occasion the story was the same. the Invaders had not broken the spirit of the Tibetan. The inner strength remained, concentrating on the real stuff, the stuff of the heart.

She stood up straight to walk in, raising her head. Her inner self would never be broken. I can do prostrations, she thought. I'll have FangFang… when he bothers to come back. And I won't be chased any more… A loving heart is too strong to be broken….

The gate clanged sharply behind her. Bang! She was taken down long, concrete corridors. As far as she was aware there was no paperwork. Just an icy silence from the Invader prison wardens, who brandished batons and electric prods. The thought of them terrified her. She knew the stories of the instruments of torture that were used regularly… The only good thing was that at least she wouldn't have to smell the Geezer-in-Black any more.

She was pushed roughly into a large room with high window slits, low box-beds around the walls and a few stinky buckets in one corner. It was full of Tibetan women in colourful but filthy chupas or tattered nun's robes. Some were gnawing on what she later discovered to be rat bones.

All her resolve to be strong broke down as they welcomed her with loving hugs. "Tashi delek," said one pretty woman with an appalling scar down the side of her face. "You can share my space, here."

Torma sat back against the wall and sobbed her heart out.

Later that afternoon they were herded out to an outside courtyard and marched around before queueing up for a thin cold liquid called soup. Torma didn't have a bowl but almost every woman shared with her. This made her cry again.

That night, the woman with the scar whispered Torma her story. "They forced me to have an operation so I couldn't have children. I was so upset I became less careful about what I said. A spy heard me say that I wish us Tibetans could run our own country. And here I am. No trial. No hope of release. One day I stood up for a woman who was being tortured." She fingered the scar on her face nervously. "Plenty of opportunity to practise being loving... Even the rats give themselves here..."

All the women insisted Torma have one of the few spaces on the box-beds. The woman with the scar curled up on the floor alongside. Torma felt as though life had taken her from a state of no mother to one of many mothers. So things had taken a strange, confusing turn. She missed the sky, and she missed FangFang. But her real worry was the torture instruments and what might lie ahead. Her dreams that night were filled with ugly implements chasing her...

So the next morning when a warden came in and pointed at her with his electric prod and shouted what can only have been "You! Out!" she trembled with fear. The women spoke loving words of encouragement as she went. She was taken to a room where she was surprised to find the two soldiers from the minivan. They nodded at the warden and then, holding her firmly on each side, marched her out of the prison gates.

"What's going on?" she asked, not sure whether to be relieved or frightened. Neither spoke. They pulled her into the backseat of a car and she was driven through the city, a city of wide streets full of lights and shops, vehicles, billboards, blaring noise, all watched over by the cameras... The people seemed to be Invaders, many of them policemen and soldiers, but now and again she spotted Tibetans skulking at corners or walking about with their heads down.

They drew up outside a posh hotel. She was taken inside and up in a lift to the fifth floor. Then along a corridor to a room which had two chairs outside. One of the soldiers unlocked the door and they all went in. It was a room with en suite, huge beds, glass chandeliers and priceless antique vases. It was the size of the prison cell she'd just left. A prison cell, but of a different sort. This one had just two people in it – the dudey aunts.

They held out their arms and hugged her tightly, but didn't jump with joy in their usual way of greeting. They had bags under their eyes and a worn, haunted look, as though they'd been through more than they'd wanted to. The soldiers went around all the windows, firmly locking them. Torma's reputation went before her.

"I'm sorry aunts…" she began. She was sure it was all her fault as usual.

"No, no," said Aunt Ani. "It's no one's fault. We're just pleased to've got you out. It wasn't easy at all. And there's something important we have to tell you. But first we have a visitor. It's Granny's cousin. She lives in the city with her pingpong family. We've managed to get permission for her to come and see us. Aunt Yuhu is very good at the bribing technique."

There was a knock on the door and the soldiers let in the hotel manager, who carried a tea tray. Not the usual thermos and bowls but a fine collector's tea-pot and cups and saucers, saved for important guests. He poured out the tea, looked around with satisfaction at his immaculate top-class guest room, and left bowing, saying in Invader English, "Have a nice day". Behind him came a small Tibetan woman who didn't look unlike Granny. It made Torma for the first time long to be back in London.

"Tashi delek," the cousin beamed, bringing her hands to her heart as Torma happily translated for the aunts, "How lovely to see you. Tell me all the news." She sat down and they all drank tea awkwardly. She looked around furtively, aware that walls have ears, and spoke quietly. "You must be Torma. How Tibetan you look," she smiled. "I can see the family resemblance."

Torma noticed Aunt Ani shifting uneasily and didn't know why.

"Please take this gift back to your granny for us."

The cousin placed on the glass table a beautiful bronze statue with blue hair. "It's my most precious possession. It belonged to your great-great-grandparents. Such a shame my parents never made it out after the invasion like your great-grandparents. We lost contact with all our family ties then. We're not permitted to leave the country. So I want this to connect us up now – across the world."

Torma nodded sadly.

"And how is life for you?" asked Aunt Yuhu. "What news can we take back to London?" The cousin looked around again, careful to choose her words. "Good. Life is good. My son is one of the lucky ones, with a job. My grandchildren are at school. We have food." Her eyes portrayed a different answer. "But our lives have meaning," she added, determined to keep positive.

Torma gave her the special chonkas from Kathmandu. It seemed right to give her a gift filled with good vibes. She wanted to keep the ones from Amala and Pala for herself. They would always connect her to them.

"Thu je che, thank you. They will be our new most treasured possessions," the cousin said, deeply touched. She rose to leave as the soldiers waited to escort her out. "It would've been nice to have invited you to our home, but sadly it's not permitted. Tashi delek."

"So…" said Aunt Ani, hesitatingly, as the door was shut and locked behind their guest.

"What did you want to tell me? Torma asked, sitting back and crossing her legs, still in the dusty red boots, comfortably under her in the immaculately clean armchair. She was hot in her

Tibetan clothes, but she certainly didn't want to change. She knew she was Tibetan. All her life she'd wanted to be certain. To belong. Now, where-ever she was in the world she would carry the Tibetan flame in her heart. She was deeply happy about that.

"It's about how we got you out of prison, Torma-la," Aunt Ani said. "You have to know."

"After we eventually arrived here, we tried using all the money we had to bribe the authorities to release you," said Aunt Yuhu. "But this time the crazy dimsims wouldn't do it." She looked at Aunt Ani anxiously.

"So we had to use the only pingpong way we could think of," said Aunt Ani. "You must understand it was the only option." She looked away from Torma, staring out of the window. There were streetlights and wires and buildings in front of a view of far-distant brown hills.

Torma waited patiently.

"We had to tell them about your father," Aunt Ani said. "The woman police chief's uncle made it possible.

Torma jumped up excitedly. "My father? What? What?"

"We had to tell them that your father was a pingpong Invader."

ANGELIC REALM

39

What Next?

"FangFang," said Honey Angel. "You must go back. Our girl needs you."

"Jumpin' jellyfish! I don't know if I can face telling her I'm the penguin. She's had enough shocks. She may never want to talk to me again."

"But you'll be able to help her. And anyway, I think you'll find she's grown. She's learned about the real values of the heart."

"Okay. I'll think about it."

"If it helps, I've been talking with the chief angels about your special case. They think that as it's not definite that you lived in the Earth Realm, then it's also not definite that you died. So if you chose to, you could have your penguin body back... Though you may be better off as you are..."

"Uh-oh!..."

"After all, in the Angelic Realm it's easy to change your appearance to whatever you would like it to be."

"Coolish! I need to sort out wings..."

"And they have an additional assignment for you if you're interested. There are three wandering little penguins whose minds haven't been awakened yet..."

"Promotion! More guiding work!"

"You deserve it. You've worked hard."

FangFang thought for a while. "And a body... The only problem is...it's in some yeti cave way off on the far side of the Himalayan mountains on the wild Tibetan plateau..." He thought some more. "At least the yeti family will be happy with that... See how compassionate I've become..."

"Yup! It's important to be compassionate to yetis, however elusive they are..."

"Janglin' angels! I guess there're worse places to leave a body hanging about..."

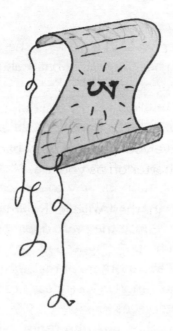

EARTH REALM

40

What We Are...

"Yes, we had to tell them that your father was an Invader," said Aunt Ani. "That, even though he met your mother in England, he was an important bigwig in the government here. That any publicity about holding his daughter in prison would look really bad."

It took a few seconds for the words to sink in. A

long few seconds.

"My father was an Invader," she said, tasting bitterness on her tongue. "That makes me half an Invader. NOoooooooo!!!"

The dam burst.

"NOoooo," she screamed, again and again. Picking up the bronze statue she threw it as hard as she could at the chandelier, scattering glass across the room on its way to a priceless antique vase, which smashed with a clatter and bounced off – Thump! – into the wall, ripping down gilded wallpaper. Then she grabbed the teapot and hurled that at another porcelain vase, which collapsed onto another priceless vase on its way to a thousand pieces.

A soldier rushed into the room, took one look and rushed out, locking the door behind him. "Coward!" shouted Aunt Yuhu.

Torma was breaking teacups onto the glass table when Aunt Ani came and put her arms tightly around her. "I hate him! I hate him!" she shouted, banging her fists furiously on Aunt Ani's chest.

Aunt Ani held her close until the rage subsided and the tears began to fall. She sobbed harder than she'd ever sobbed on the mountain or in prison. Her heart, like the antique vases, was broken into a thousand pieces.

Aunt Ani rocked her gently, holding an egg-of-light around her. And explained, "Your father was a good man. He was trying to bring reform to the pingpong Invaders. To treat Tibetans differently. But they wouldn't listen to him... He couldn't tell anyone he had a Tibetan family in London. It would've made things impossible for him."

"What happened to him?" Torma sniffled, somehow already knowing the answer.

"He disappeared. The official view was that he had an unfortunate car accident and was honoured as a hero of the motherland. But we believe he died in prison...died for trying to bring people together...or trying to make the world a better place. He was a great warrior of the heart, Torma-la. You can be proud of him."

"But I don't look like an Invader," she said, still not wanting to believe it was true. Though the ocean of pain she was in told her it was.

"No, but your mother looked very Tibetan. I think she died of a broken heart, when she couldn't stop your father going back. She loved him very much. And you have your granny's Tibetan ways."

Torma nodded.

"Love is more important than what we are..."

She hugged Aunt Ani.

Aunt Yuhu crunched through the wreck of the room, surveying the devastation with a wry smile. There was a little bit of her that would have liked to have done this too, but she couldn't dare think thoughts like that until tomorrow, when they would hopefully be safely out of the country.

She picked up the bronze statue, the only thing which seemed to be unharmed. It was as beautiful as ever, except underneath there was a small leather hatch that had come open. She passed it to Torma.

"Here, look. I think you ought to be the one to open this. Whatever is inside has been there for a very long time."

Torma peered in at the treasure. She pulled out bundles of seeds and herbs wrapped in browned cloth. It smelled musty. And then out came two tiny scrolls. The first was of mottled parchment tied with the string that monks wear around their wrists.

She looked at the aunts, who urged her to open it. Carefully she unrolled it, the edges crumbling. Brushing away some of the shards of glass on the battered table, she was able to spread it out, holding it either side. Words were painted on it in beautiful Tibetan calligraphy with an exquisite border of intricate patterns and figures.

The second was of paper which looked to be torn from a book and held English writing as though someone had thought it important to add the translation of the first scroll at a later date. They stared at it:

There was a prophesy, heralded by a blood-red sky, that our land would be stolen by foreigners and our people violated and crushed... We must suffer the resulting pain that runs through our souls because somehow we have the strength to suffer this. So could it be that this deep pain gives us a tremendous strength with which to help the world in its growth? A heart growth that is needed to survive...

"What do you think it means?" asked Aunt Yuhu.

Torma didn't hesitate. "I think it means pain makes us strong. And then we can help others."

Aunt Yuhu looked at Torma with new respect. "Torma-la, that's true. You've grown wise.

"Also," said Aunt Ani, "I believe it's a pingpong call to Tibetans to keep on fighting the greed and violence of the world with compassion. The Tibetan heart does this as its service."

Yay! thought Torma. I'll be able to give Tenzin the scroll and tell him that the heart of Tibet still beats. I've seen compassion in the toughest of places, like the women in the prison and with Amala and Pala on the kora – they'll still be my parents in my mind, even though I'll probably never see them again. But more. I'll be able to tell Tenzin that the magic heart of Tibet is even now helping the world. And most of all…that I, Torma, intend to always be part of it.

Thank goodness I've cracked that answer, her thoughts continued, 'cos I've failed dismally on the other part of my quest – to find the lost penguin.

At least she was able to be reunited with Speak Peace and Think Peace, and happily curled up to sleep with them on blankets in the bath, the only space free of sharp shards of glass. Things were less dangerous in prison!

The following morning they prepared to leave. The manager of the hotel didn't see them off. He was busy doing something else. But the soldiers took them to the airport and through a special military security process to find their seats quickly. They told the cabin crew that under no circumstances should that quiet little girl in Tibetan clothes be left behind, for she was a national security threat.

They were given their things which had been confiscated on coming into the country. Torma received back her book on troublesome yetis, Aunt Yuhu the tennis ball, which was obviously too dangerous an item to leave behind, and the

cameras.

After the plane had taken off they enjoyed looking at all the earlier pictures in Nepal. "Look," said Aunt Ani. So many of them have got those lovely magic circles in. That indicates that we had angels with us all along."

Coolish! came the voice only Torma could hear.

"FangFang! Where on Earth have you been?"

Nope, not on Earth, he said in an enigmatic, angel way.

"And you're able to speak on planes!"

Uh-oh!... I'm an experienced invisible guide now.

"Well, I'm an Invader."

I know that. I listened in.

"But I've learned that it doesn't matter what you are... It's the love in your heart that counts."

I know that too.

"How d'you know that?"

Because I'm a penguin.

"You're a penguin!?"

Jumpin' jellyfish! I'm the penguin you've been looking for all along...

"Idiot! No way... I don't believe you."

Torma settled down in her seat cuddling Speak Peace and Think Peace. Go across the mountains to look for a penguin? Yay! No problem. Though, good idea to bring your own...

She looked out of the window at the Earth

below. The great Himalayan range stretched into the distance, gleaming white in the morning sun. It reminded her she'd soon have ice cream again.

And there was work to be done. She had a lot of trees to plant.

Watch out for your inner yeti —
seeing all things as you would
love to see them...

Soft
Courage

Tess
Burrows

A true-life fable: Discovering wisdom through adventure

Yannick, the soft-toy penguin who accompanies Tess Burrows on all her extreme adventures, tells us about them from his particular perspective. He has absorbed some of the teachings that have inspired Tess herself, and his own inner journey unfolds during his extensive travels with Tess. In his simple way, Yannick reminds us of the things that matter most.

ISBN: 9781785630170

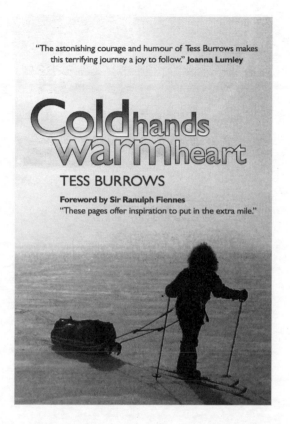

"The astonishing courage and humour of Tess Burrows makes this terrifying journey a joy to follow." **Joanna Lumley**

Coldhands warmheart

TESS BURROWS

Foreword by Sir Ranulph Fiennes
"These pages offer inspiration to put in the extra mile."

Old-age pensioners Tess and Pete journey across the coldest, driest, windiest place on Earth, with the intent of reaching the South Pole to read out peace messages collected from people from around the world. Their mission was to promote peace on Earth, and Tess charts their highs and lows as they haul themselves and their kit across the Antarctic continent in pursuit of it.

ISBN: 9781903070789

We share in Tess' experience of the vibrancy and colour of Africa as the gutsy and compassionate grandmother takes on Kilimanjaro, the highest mountain on the continent. For this peace climb, as a metaphor for people pulling together, she drags with her a tyre filled with peace messages, but can she make it to the top of a mountain that defeats sixty per cent of those who attempt it?

ISBN: 9781903070895

FOREWORD BY THE DALAI LAMA
INTRODUCTION BY JOANNA LUMLEY

EYE CLASSICS

CRY FROM THE HIGHEST
MOUNTAIN – TESS BURROWS

20TH ANNIVERSARY EDITION

Tess Burrows sets off on a spiritual mountaineering mission
to climb to the highest place on Earth – 2,000 metres higher
than Everest – to broadcast thousands of peace messages in
support of the Tibetan people. No one expects it to be easy,
but the extreme challenge to both body and mind pushes
Tess towards the ultimate point within herself as she nears
the ultimate point on Earth, relative to the planetary core.

ISBN: 9781785631153

About the Author

Tess Burrows is the first granny to race to the South Pole. She is an extreme adventurer and peace campaigner, who has gone to the very limits to pursue her mission of promoting peace on Earth. She has sent off thousands of messages, many written by children, from the North and South Poles, the Himalayas, the Andes, the Pacific and Africa, raising over £157,000 for charity.

Don't Blame the Yeti is based on her personal journey hiking across the Himalayas, up through north-west Nepal, into Tibet and around Mount Kailas – undertaking prostrations.

Proceeds from this book go towards Tibetan causes supported by **climbfortibet.org**.
See also **tessburrows.org**.

"No matter what people call you,
you are just who you are…"
THE DALAI LAMA